Her Fri

Paul Tos

This is a work of fiction. Similarities to real people, places, or events are entirely coincidental.

HER FRIENDS

First edition. October 27, 2024.

Copyright © 2024 Paul Toskiam.

ISBN: 978-2959521911

Written by Paul Toskiam.

Also by Paul Toskiam

The Curse of Patosia Bay
Le bus de la peur
The fear bus
Elle mord les Zombies !
She Bites Zombies
No Treasure for the Brave
Pas de Trésor pour les Braves
Black Stone Hunter
Chasseur de Pierres Noires
Le Destin de Lucian
The Fate of Lucian
Her Friends

Warning

This book is a work of fiction. The names, characters, places, and incidents are products of the author's imagination and are used fictitiously. Any resemblance to actual persons, living or dead, events, or locations is entirely coincidental.

This book should not be used as a source of information or advice. The author and the publisher of this novel accept no responsibility for any damage caused by the reading of this novel.

This novel is intended for adults who have reached the age of legal majority in the country of purchase, and contains scenes that may be shocking to some readers.

Copyright © 2024 by Paul Toskiam.

All rights reserved. No part of this book may be reproduced, distributed, or transmitted in any form or by any means, including photocopying, recording, or other electronic or mechanical methods, now known or hereafter invented, without the prior written permission of the author, except in the case of brief quotations incorporated in reviews and certain other non-commercial uses permitted by copyright law.

The Plumber

Justine and Lydia's Apartment

"Mom, the plumber is here!"

On this Saturday morning, Justine was still fighting the grip of sleep. For the past few weeks, her nights had been restless, caught in a vise of devouring nightmares. Fatigue, like a heavy blanket, weighed down on her this morning, holding her at the threshold of dreams and reality.

Lydia, her thirteen-year-old daughter, burst into the dimness of her mother's room. She found, half-surprised, Justine still lying down, her feet barely touching the floor as if she had been drawn out of bed. Her daughter's call startled her, pulling her painfully from unconsciousness. "Damn... already?" she mumbled, as she rubbed her eyes still clouded with sleep.

Lydia, mixing disappointment and concern in her voice, gently advised her, "Stop doing that, Mom, it's bad for your eyes." She left the room, leaving Justine in a state of semi-awakening.

For several weeks, Justine had been grappling with tormented nights marked by haunting and anxious dreams. She had shared her struggles with her doctor, who simply prescribed her some pills to help her sleep better.

Justine laboriously propped herself up and hurried to the restroom to relieve her oppressed bladder. She pressed her hands against her feverish forehead as Lydia timidly approached the corner of the door.

"Are you okay, Mom?" Lydia asked, concern piercing her youthful voice.

Justine, her head in her hands, replied with difficulty, "Yes, I'm fine. Where is he?"

HER FRIENDS

"In the kitchen. I opened the cupboard under the sink for him," Lydia answered while snapping a picture of her mother for posterity. The mention of the kitchen seemed to plunge Justine into an abyss of confusion. "The kitchen..." she murmured, rising unsteadily. Worried, Lydia insisted, a shiver of uncertainty running through her, "Mom, are you sure everything's alright?"

Justine finally responded in a strange tone, as if she were perceiving an invisible reality: "He was there, in the kitchen!" Her words resonated like an enigma, hinting at a mysterious dimension that defied any rational explanation. This time, Lydia felt fear: she had never seen her mom with that look, as if possessed.

PAUL TOSKIAM

Where is Sara?

George Blisken's House

George wiped the sweat from his forehead and stretched his achy muscles as he closed the front door behind him. He had spent hours under the scorching sun planting seeds, weeding, and trimming bushes. Gardening was demanding work, but he loved taking care of his little slice of paradise.

As he made his way to the bathroom to freshen up, a noise from the kitchen stopped him in his tracks.

A pot had just fallen, followed by a dull rumble. His breath caught as his mind raced through a thousand possible explanations. He slowly approached the kitchen, his heart pounding unreasonably fast for a man of his age.

When he cautiously opened the door, he was stunned by what he saw.

A colossal figure stood in the middle of the room, its pitch-black eyes fixed on him. It was a gaze mixed with fear and aggression. Its armor was dirty and worn, as if it had endured numerous battles and absorbed all sorts of brutal blows. Its long black hair was braided into a thick plait that cascaded down to its feet. George had never seen such attire. Yet, he had traveled around the globe and had seen his fair share of originals.

"Wh... Who are you?" he stammered, his voice trembling.

The colossal being straightened up, almost touching the ceiling, and a sinister smile stretched across its lips. "I am Admiral Mobo. I am looking for Sara," it replied in a deep, powerful voice that made the dishes in the cabinets tremble and the old, poorly insulated windows rattle. He had a rough wheeze at the end of his sentence, followed by a slight hiss, as if his lungs were battling with phlegm. George was a retired doctor. He could recognize chronic bronchitis just by the sound.

This attentive listening didn't prevent him from feeling a wave of intense terror wash over him from head to toe. What could this guy possibly want in this quiet suburban house?

He tried to keep his cool and asked in a voice he hoped sounded firm, "How did you get in here?"

The giant chuckled, making a sound worn down by years of cruelty. "Sara possesses the power. I came to find her," he said, taking a step forward and bowing his head to avoid scraping the ceiling.

Trying to hide his visceral fear, George observed him, fascinated by his oversized dimensions. He must have weighed tons, as the floor tiles cracked beneath his feet. The slight creaking sound on each tile, followed by crushed sand, was characteristic of immense mechanical pressure.

George straightened up, fueled by a sudden wave of courage: "Get out! Leave or I'll call the police!" he threatened in a warrior's spasm, puffing out his elderly chest to intimidate the opponent. The elderly can be bold.

He didn't quite understand what was happening in his home. He was trying to handle this exceptionally extraordinary situation with ordinary means—and his perception of the world—while his mind had no reference points or reflexes to effectively face it.

Irritated, Admiral Mobo slammed his fist into the nearest wall, which crumbled in a deafening crash. A cloud of dust filled the space, leaving a gaping opening to the living room.

This noise was followed by a long silence during which the dust swirled until it completely concealed the giant's immense silhouette. George still looked in his direction, petrified with fear, but his fists were clenched. As the dust began to settle, he first caught sight of the dark, predatory gaze of the giant, staring at him like the barrel of a gun ready

HER FRIENDS

to fire. With a flick of his hand, Admiral Mobo brushed away the debris and part of the ceiling that had fallen on him, as if fixing his hair. He let out an exasperated sigh. "You don't understand, old man. You can do nothing against me. I am powerful, and I will do whatever it takes to get what I want. Where... is... Sara...?"

Mobo slowly advanced toward George, the tiles creaking under his weight with each of his powerful, deep steps. George thought quickly. He needed to find a way to protect her from this monster who was beginning to destroy his home right in front of him. He thought of his daughter's room, which had been vacant for years. The photos of his beloved daughter, smiling and innocent, were still there, in their frames. Had Admiral Mobo already searched that room? George found it hard to imagine this colossal being sifting through his daughter's personal belongings. Everything was jumbled and crashing in his mind.

He proposed a pitiful bargain to Admiral Mobo, hoping to divert him from his sinister intent. "If I show you Sara's room and give you her photos, will you leave us alone?" he said randomly, running out of inspiration.

Admiral Mobo stopped abruptly and chuckled again. But this time, a glimmer of interest flickered in his dark, aggressive eyes. "Show me the room, and maybe I will be merciful," he said, closing his fist as if crushing something fragile.

George looked away, unable to hold the gaze of this malevolent being any longer. "Wait for me just a moment, I'll grab the key to her room and take you there," he stammered, not waiting for a response.

He thought intensely about his daughter and rushed to the back of the entrance. His hands trembled as he opened the door of the cupboard under the stairs to grab his old rifle and some cartridges. He loaded it in a hurry, accidentally dropping two cartridges in the process. He paused and looked up to listen, fearing that the monster had caught on to his plans. But he only heard the wheezing of that sickly breathing in response. He inhaled all the oxygen he could and dashed down the hallway, rushing toward the kitchen and shaking the small drawer in the entrance with its beautiful antique vase that tipped over. It was the gift Sara had just given him for his birthday.

Back at the open kitchen door, he planted himself with his legs slightly apart to lower his center of gravity and aimed at the giant's head.

"TAKE THIS, SON OF A BITCH!" he yelled, pulling the trigger on two cartridges at once.

George trembled with every fiber of his being as he reloaded both barrels before firing again. The recoil had thrown him off balance, and he took a few seconds to discover Mobo's bloodied face. The Admiral's eyes were still fixed on him, unmoving, without a blink, almost silent, except for his hoarse, wheezing breath at the end of exhalation.

George had aimed true, right at the face. But the muscle mountain before him remained impassive, and he was out of ammunition. He felt helpless and, most importantly, at the mercy of this stranger who could crush him with a mere gesture. His desperate attempt had worn out all his bravery and the remnants of his strength. Yet, he had barely scratched the colossus.

"All you want are those photos?" George asked in a weak voice, though his mind still scheming.

"I want what you offered me, old man," Mobo replied with a wheeze that seemed never-ending.

George led the Admiral through the dim hallway to his daughter's room door. Mobo bent and twisted delicately. Miraculously, he fit through everywhere. The old man paused, his hand trembling on the doorknob.

"Promise me you won't harm her," he asked in a weakened voice, as if pleading. He had no reason or desire to trust this intruder, impressive as he was. But did he really have a choice?

HER FRIENDS

Admiral Mobo nodded, marking his impatience. His unsettling smile returned to his lips. "I came to protect her," he said in a tone reminiscent of a lion's roar, moving volumes of air around him.

Frightened and not understanding the stranger's true motivation, George pushed open the door to his daughter's room and was, as always, overwhelmed by a wave of nostalgic memories. The walls were still covered with posters, but time had dulled their brilliance. He walked toward the desk where a frame held a special photo. Sara beamed up at him, jumping in the air. The photo was from her last year in this house. He gently brushed away the dust covering the glass with his shirt sleeve and offered it to Admiral Mobo, presenting it as a gift.

The colossal being took the photo frame in his immense hands. His gaze lingered on Sara's smiling face. He slowly grazed the image with the curve of his hooked index nail. A light of sadness flickered in his dark, abyss-like eyes. Finally, he handed the photo back to George.

"You have fulfilled your part of the bargain," he said in an unexpectedly calm voice, almost soothing. "Take this."

Before George could respond, Admiral Mobo vanished, as if he had melted into the very air, in a gust that slammed all doors and windows shut.

The old man stood frozen for a long moment in the bedroom, unable to make sense of what he had just experienced. His still trembling hands awkwardly held a stone, the size of an egg, that resembled a diamond.

PAUL TOSKIAM

Admiral Mobo

Flagship

Admiral Mobo stood firm, unflinching. His face, seemingly impassive, nonetheless betrayed the inner turmoil gnawing at his mind. Standing before a massive bay window, his eyes were fixed on a tiny point in the infinite expanse of space, a point that slowly grew larger. Suddenly, the Grand Master, impatient and authoritative, broke the silence with his booming voice, shattering the stillness like a merciless alarm that jolts you abruptly from your reverie.

"Admiral Mobo! Stop standing there with your mouth hanging open. What do you propose?"

In a determined tone, Mobo replied, "I recommend a massive strike on the activation sites I mentioned, to catch them off guard."

The Grand Master, with a subtle disdain, retorted, "Admiral Mobo, I expect a more direct and efficient solution from you."

Mobo hesitated for a moment before responding, "But Grand Master, do we want to kill her before we have the chance to capture her?"

"And so what?" bellowed the Grand Master, causing the throne room to tremble. "I couldn't care less if she lives or dies. All we want is her DNA, correct?"

Admiral Mobo nodded reluctantly, "That's true, Grand Master, you are right."

"You're nothing but a weak little being!" the Grand Master commented with a smug smile. Then he leaned forward, and his smile took on a predatory edge: "Have you fallen under the magical spell of this young human, Mobo?"

Mobo lowered his head, hesitating before responding, "By following her, I have developed a certain attachment, Grand Master."

The Grand Master raised an eyebrow. "So much so that you defied my order not to intervene physically?"

"I deeply regret it, Grand Master. This impulse was stronger than I am."

The Grand Master fixed him with an intense gaze, searching for a punishment. "Admiral Mobo, I want her DNA immediately. You have disobeyed my orders, and what's more, you returned empty-handed. If I came in person to this insignificant colony, it was solely for this new form of DNA detected by our sages. This sample will allow us to make a technological leap of which you have no idea," he concluded, staring into the infinite void of space as if seeking the ultimate truth.

"I understand the value of this human, Grand Master, which is why I wanted to preserve her," Admiral Mobo justified himself once more.

"Nonsense! I am taking this mission away from you and assigning it to Admiral Struiz. His methods will be swifter than your endless procrastinations," he shouted in a sudden fit of impatience and fury.

"I understand, Grand Master. Thank you for giving me the opportunity to work on this crucial mission, until now."

The Grand Master looked away with disdain: "Admiral Mobo, you exhaust me. Disappear."

Admiral Mobo left the throne room, the weight of worry heavy on his shoulders. He had once been a favorite of the Grand Master, but that time seemed long past.

The Grand Master had recently taken the young Struiz under his wing, a recruit fresh out of naval school. Struiz was one of those ambitious types who had devoured the manual "How to Colonize a Planet for Dummies" and reproduced its content mechanically, passing it off as creativity and ingenuity. Mobo found him even more unbearable because he belonged to the pioneering generation, those who had crafted the strategies contained in those manuals. How many

HER FRIENDS

worlds had he conquered for the Grand Master over the millennia? How many priceless resources had he gathered to ensure the survival of their species? He bitterly felt the unenviable fate of those who pave the way. Their feats were first mocked, then feared, and ultimately became taken for granted, a mere commodity. Mobo found his slim pride in having been part of the early ones. Future generations would know prosperity, in part thanks to him. That was his only consolation.

The Grand Master himself showed signs of aging, and each day brought a share of contenders eager to replace him. Young and brimming with confidence, they all believed they could conquer New Worlds and change the order of things. This force of youth, constantly renewed, was unstoppable.

Admiral Mobo quickly returned to his opulent quarters as a high dignitary, ignoring proposals for activities and any assistance from his synthetic staff. He isolated himself in his office, with the door closed.

With a gesture, he summoned the image of that vibrant young woman in front of him. He leaned forward, almost bent over, to observe her from all angles, a straw between his lips. He continued this meticulous study for long moments, occasionally sipping from his fizzy drink with a wheezing gasp. His eyes were fixed on this image, at times bulging, fascinated and moist. She exuded an airy grace, a devastating smile, and a sharp, mischievous spirit, occupying all the space and all his attention. She was his obsession.

Mentally, he dictated a message: "SARA, YOU ARE IN DANGER."

These words appeared in large letters in the middle of the room. Mobo hesitated for a few seconds. He reread each word as if sealing a fate. Then, with a disheartened wave of his hand, he sent the message.

PAUL TOSKIAM

Gadgetta

Gadgetta's premises

Sara had arrived early for her first day at the new company, Gadgetta. Specializing in the creation of electronic accessories, the company offered an eclectic range of products, whether they were luminous, vibrating, sound-producing, or flying. Objects that were decidedly frivolous, yet somehow indispensable in their frivolity.

Her position as purchasing manager would require her to negotiate massive quantities of these gadgets and establish contracts with suppliers. On this first day filled with enthusiasm and naivety, she patiently waited in front of the large glass window, just across from the elevators, at the reception on the seventeenth floor. However, no one seemed to pay her any attention, despite her efforts to stand out.

She observed some of her future colleagues strolling by, their expressions focused, folders tucked under their arms. A smile spread across her face. She was quite familiar with the tactic of holding folders under one's arm to project a studious and dedicated image while moving through the office. A classic. She recalled other tricks, like holding a phone to her ear even when not on a call. Or carrying a laptop with a stack of folders clutched in one arm, to create the impression that a crucial meeting couldn't commence without her. She quickly understood that at Gadgetta, appearances mattered. The formal attire of her soon-to-be colleagues also seemed to be the norm here, which made her smile again. "The more frivolities you sell, the more seriously you take yourself," she thought, growing increasingly tired of waiting.

She couldn't shake the acute longing for her vacation, and the idea of starting this new job didn't particularly excite her. Yet, deep down, she knew it was a rare opportunity. Many other candidates were still wondering what had gone wrong with their applications. Like many of her friends, she had left behind the years of madness. The frenzy of youth, and the tyranny of hormones where every action was dictated by the desire to conclude: "And in the end, do I get laid?" She remembered the nights spent exploring all substances available on the market, often in undocumented blends. Days without eating, sleeping, or vomiting, depending on the combinations and dosages. All of this had given way to a lack of ambition for the future, nearly depressing. Unwittingly, she was adhering to that very trendy simplistic precept: live in the moment. The future became an abstract, vague notion, almost quantum. And the past was just a mistake.

She thought of her father, George, as he had just left several messages on her phone. He must be worried about whether everything was going well. She would read them later. Finally, the receptionist, Olivia, noticed her and, with a warm gesture, invited her to enter by opening the glass doors. Sara returned her smile and cautiously approached the glass doors, awkwardly fearing she might bump into them. However, the motion sensors were very sensitive. As soon as she moved, the doors gracefully opened, officially marking her entry for her first day at Gadgetta.

Olivia, the young blonde receptionist, exuded a radiant aura of joy, as if she were living the best time of her life and that being a receptionist was the pinnacle of her existence.

"Hello, are you Sara?" she asked. "I'm Olivia."

"Hello Olivia. I'm delighted to meet you. Yes, I'm really early," she replied, glancing discreetly around her.

Olivia reassured her kindly, "Don't worry, everyone here is very nice. You're going to make friends, I'm sure," intercepting the anxious glances of the new recruit.

Olivia confirmed her ten o'clock appointment with the boss, Paul, in his office. Curious to explore the premises before their meeting, Sara

HER FRIENDS

politely asked, "Excuse me, could you tell me where the restroom is? I'd like to go before my appointment."

A warm smile instinctively spread across Olivia's face. She replied in a low voice, "Oh, I totally understand! On the first day, I also feel the urge. It's nerve-wracking, don't worry. The restrooms are just over there, to the left, near the coffee machine."

Thanking Olivia, she headed towards the restroom, appreciating the friendliness of her colleague at reception. She loved straightforward and honest people and felt pleased to have already met one in this new company.

When she reached the restroom, she was immediately dazzled. A flash of light escaped from the cracks of the entrance door. This beam of light, streaming around the doorframe, was so intense that it illuminated the whole hallway. Blinded, she shut her eyes too late and found that the outline of the door had imprinted on her retina. What kind of magic was producing such intensity of light? Intrigued, she moved closer to check when the door opened in front of her.

"Oh, excuse me! Sorry!" she exclaimed upon encountering the young man exiting the restroom.

"It's nothing," he said with a broad smile, realizing he had startled her. "You're Sara?"

"Yes, Sara Blisken, the new purchasing manager," she replied in a very professional tone.

"Hello, I'm Paul Lessep, and I run this company. Welcome to Gadgetta. I'll be working directly with you. I'm glad to meet you in person. I've heard great things about you," he congratulated her warmly.

She felt relieved to see how welcoming Paul was. She replied enthusiastically, "Thank you, that's very kind. I'm also looking forward to working with you and contributing to the success of the business."

This was her way of comforting herself in front of important strangers: showering them with compliments, generously. Paul extended his hand with all fingers spread apart. She had already noticed this way of shaking hands. It was often a sign of excessive self-confidence, coupled with a complete lack of contradiction in life. It was a trait of winners or manic individuals. She paid close attention to little details, the signs that spoke volumes. She accepted the firm and benevolent handshake, still slightly damp. Once he left, she would go wash her hands again. She had kept in mind the stories of her grandmother who used to say that all men just urinated on their hands and never really washed them afterward. But Grandma didn't like men. She had ended up disliking them after several disappointments.

"I'll see you at 10 o'clock in my office?" he asked, well aware of the answer. "I'm sure we're going to have a great day. See you later!" he said with an encouraging smile.

"Absolutely, see you later! Thanks again, Sir," she replied, completely using up her first tube of ointment. No regrets. Paul, as her boss, fully deserved it!

She watched him stride down the hallway, energetic and loud. He wore small metal tips on the pointed heels of his shoes, like the winners.

But what could have caused that dazzling light that had burst out from inside the restroom?

The incident piqued her curiosity, and a slight worry began to creep in. Had she really seen that light? Or was it a hallucination? A mirage?

After careful thought, she decided to keep this incident to herself. She awaited more insights about her new boss. And for that, she already had a good ally.

She shook her head slightly, as if to dispel those thoughts, and focused on her meeting with Paul. She expected a logical explanation.

As she returned to the reception area, she noticed Olivia waiting for her with interest, wearing a knowing smile. "So?" she asked, her smile spreading to her eyes.

Olivia seemed to know more than she wanted to let on.

"So what?" Sara replied, curious.

HER FRIENDS

"Oh, don't play innocent. I can see everything from here, you know?" Olivia explained, discreetly indicating the row of surveillance camera screens behind her desk.

She realized with astonishment that Olivia had witnessed the whole scene in the restroom through the cameras. Suspicious, she wondered if this situation had been orchestrated in advance without her knowledge.

"Well... about that light in the restroom..." she stammered, testing the waters on the topic with Olivia, who was eagerly waiting.

"Yes! Did you see the flash of light? Did you notice how intense and dazzling it was?" Olivia asked with a hint of excitement, eager to get all the details she might have missed on the control screens.

"That's right. For a brief moment, I was blinded. It was like a flash," she explained with round gestures in the air, unable to provide more details.

Olivia smiled, conspiratorial, as if they now shared a well-kept secret.

"Here's your badge," said Olivia, handing the object over with a warm smile. "Don't forget to keep it close. We wouldn't want you to get fired so soon," she added, sparking a shared laugh between them.

Sara chuckled heartily, though it wasn't particularly funny. She had learned to laugh at others' humor, mechanically, to put them at ease.

Olivia's tone was playful, and her warm gaze showed she was joking amicably and sincerely. The badge displayed the company's logo, a kind of dragon with powerful engines beneath its wings. A logo for winners. She accepted the badge while mimicking the act of biting it with her teeth—like athletes do with medals—and thanked Olivia for her warm, seemingly selfless welcome.

"Don't worry, I'll take good care of it! I'm so happy to be here and to be part of this amazing team," she declared in a professional and mechanical tone to express her gratitude.

Olivia nodded with a satisfied smile. "It's great to hear you say that. I'm sure you're going to thrive here. If you need any help or anything, don't hesitate to let me know, okay?" she offered, echoing Sara's gracious tone.

The reason for this scripted exchange was that Paul had quietly approached the reception area and was observing their friendly interaction, like a wolf among sheep.

"Thank you, Olivia, that's very kind of you. I won't hesitate to reach out if needed," she replied to show her appreciation. The two women exchanged a knowing smile while Paul gestured with a winner's wave, inviting Sara to follow him to his office.

But when her gaze met his, fixed on her intensely as if she were a dessert at the end of a meal, she stood frozen, unable to move.

"Well?" Paul said, smiling ear to ear.

She regained her composure and nodded, returning the smile with a slight tilt of her head, then followed him through the corridors.

As she tried to put her badge away in her jacket pocket, she noticed it was accompanied by a small handwritten note stuck to it: "Shall we have lunch together at noon?" It was a little message that Olivia had discreetly slipped to her.

She smiled upon reading the note, touched by this friendly invitation. She felt lucky to have found such camaraderie on her first day of work.

"Sit wherever you like," Paul offered, gesturing towards the large round table. He watched her hesitate for a few seconds in front of the table before sinking into his large brown leather armchair.

She was discovering Paul's office, which had a very minimalist style.

His minimalist style gave an impression of calm and serenity. The walls were immaculate white, without any paintings or unnecessary decorations. The furniture was simple and functional, with straight lines and high-quality materials. Everything was perfectly tidy and organized. The only colors came from the green plants scattered here

HER FRIENDS

and there, adding a touch of life to the whole. She felt at peace in this minimalist environment, as if Paul's office were a haven of tranquility amidst the chaos of the outside world.

She chose the chair opposite Paul's desk and settled in front of him. Suddenly, she looked up and locked eyes with Paul. A ray of sunlight hit near his eyes, revealing a deep ocean blue. He seemed to have been scrutinizing her for a while with an unsettling intensity. She felt as though she were being examined under a microscope.

Without saying a word, he slowly rose from his chair and approached her.

He was tall and elegant, wearing a dark suit that highlighted his athletic figure. His face was marked by a light stubble, giving him a simultaneously mysterious and attractive air. She had to admit to herself that he was in a league of unattainable beauty. Normally, she enjoyed attracting handsome men. But the gap separating her from him intimidated her: it wasn't just a gap, but a canyon. Looking more closely, he was a sort of absolute manifestation of beauty: an animated ancient statue. She was unsettled by these thoughts, and she didn't like it at all.

He stopped in front of her, almost within breath's reach, and plunged his gaze into hers. She perceived him as a predator circling around her, ready to pounce. She shifted slightly, overwhelmed by a wave of contradictory emotions, a mix of curiosity and apprehension.

Still silent, Paul began to assess her from head to toe. His eyes traveled over every curve of her body, lingering on each detail. She suddenly felt a blush of embarrassment, as if she were exposed in front of everyone. She wondered what could fascinate him so much. A guy built like him must be used to women.

The silence felt really heavy. Yet she couldn't tear her gaze away from Paul's. She was locked onto him. She felt her heart racing like a marathon runner's, her cheeks flushing. She wanted to ask him why he was looking at her like that for several minutes, but the words stuck in her throat and wouldn't come out.

Finally, Paul broke the silence. His voice was soft and deep, resonating in the charged atmosphere. "You're stunning," he said simply. She was taken aback by this unexpected statement. She didn't know how to respond, but something inside her told her she could trust him.

"Thank you," she murmured, almost shyly, a smile beginning to form on her lips. She felt more at ease, as if Paul's gaze was dispelling all her fears.

Eventually, Paul extended his hand towards her. "Would you like to have a coffee with me?" he proposed with a charming smile. She hesitated for a moment, but deep down she knew she couldn't resist this intense connection. At least, not on her first day.

"Yes," she replied, her hand slipping into his.

Paul approached the coffee machine in his office and prepared two steaming cups. He carefully picked them up, making sure not to spill a single drop. He approached her with a confident smile, ready to offer her this welcoming drink.

Standing before him, she looked at him with interest in return. He knew how to make an impression, that guy. She wondered what this coffee break could reveal about Paul, this mysterious man who already intrigued her so much.

She was meeting Paul for the first time, sharing this moment with him. Her interviews had been with other colleagues. She had anticipated meeting a mature man, the one she had seen online. Apparently, it was the son she should have in front of her.

Paul delicately placed the cups on the table, making sure to align them well. He sat next to her, their knees almost brushing. He handed her a cup, their fingers briefly grazing during the exchange. She felt a shiver surge through her, traveling up her arm to her neck, then down

HER FRIENDS

her spine to her lower back. She made a small discreet movement to release this excess energy.

"Thank you," she replied, smiling. Her eyes sparkled with gratitude. For reasons she couldn't quite grasp, she felt light as air, ready to soar across the room.

As he handed her the coffee cup, Paul's hands trembled slightly, revealing his nervousness. She noticed, but said nothing, thinking it might be a form of magic between them.

However, at the moment she grabbed the coffee cup, a clumsy gesture from Paul caused it to tip over, spilling hot liquid onto the table and on her white suit. A sharp cry of surprise escaped her lips, and she stood up abruptly, trying to shield herself from the scalding coffee that was still pouring over her.

"I'm sorry! Really sorry!" Paul exclaimed, visibly embarrassed by his clumsiness.

She tried to remain calm despite the warmth of the coffee on her skin. She attempted to wipe the spilled coffee from her clothes, but it was already too late. The coffee had spread, forming a constellation of stains. She felt uncomfortable in this awkward situation.

"It's nothing," she replied, trying to downplay the incident. "These are just accidents that happen."

Paul quickly searched for tissues and towels to help her clean up the mess, and Olivia, who had heard Sara's cry, rushed into the office.

"What happened?" she asked, concerned.

Paul also apologized to Olivia, awkwardly explaining the situation. Olivia smiled, shaking her head. "Don't worry, Paul. It happens to everyone. Wait here, I'll go get some towels to clean this up," she said kindly as she exited the room.

Together, they cleaned the office and reassured Sara, who managed to keep a polite smile despite the incident. The collective embarrassment gradually faded away, replaced by a more relaxed atmosphere as the three of them joked about this funny situation.

"Still sorry," Paul repeated, visibly embarrassed.

"He does this to every new recruit!" Olivia chimed in playfully.

She smiled kindly. "Don't worry about it, really. It's a memorable way to start my first day here," she said to ease Paul's concerns.

He picked up his own cup and blew gently on the hot liquid before taking a sip. "Mine survived. Let's not waste it!" he said, looking intensely at Sara, as if trying to read her thoughts.

She noticed his piercing gaze once again and felt both vulnerable and attracted to him. She wondered what he was really thinking at that moment, what he felt. She wondered if he felt the same inexplicable, sudden connection.

"Paul, I'm really happy to have the opportunity to work here," she declared, trying to move past the coffee incident.

Paul smiled, his eyes shining with approval. "I'm glad to hear that. I think you're going to bring a lot to the table."

She looked at him, raising her eyebrows slightly. He noticed and continued, "I think you're going to contribute a lot to our teams. I'm certain of it."

She felt encouraged by his words, a growing sense of confidence within her. He really seemed kind and helpful. But she knew well that it was just a façade. All very attractive guys are twisted and troubled in their heads. Life is so easy for them. Only twisted things bring them pleasure. She was just waiting for the moment he would drop the mask. The moment when the carriage would turn back into a pumpkin.

"Paul, I was really intrigued earlier by that dazzling light I saw in the bathroom," she confessed to test him.

A sly smile spread across Paul's face.

"Oh, that's a little secret at Gadgetta," he replied enigmatically. But he didn't seem surprised at all.

She tilted her head slightly, like a small pet in front of a treat, curious to learn the truth.

"A secret?" she asked.

HER FRIENDS

Paul took another sip of coffee, savoring the moment of suspense. "Well, you see, that light is actually a technology we're developing here at Gadgetta. We call it 'the light in your underwear.'"

Her eyes widened. It was indeed she who was taken aback by this unexpected revelation. "The light in your underwear? What does that mean?" she asked, almost choking on her words.

Paul chuckled softly, enjoying the confusion he had just concocted. "It's a technology that allows for integrating high-power LEDs into underwear. It creates a soft and soothing light or, conversely, intense and energetic brightness. It's perfect for adding a touch of fun at night."

She couldn't help but burst into laughter. "That's really original! I never would have imagined a company could develop such technology. I mean, so brilliant!" Yet she thought to herself, "Come on, do you really think I'm that gullible?" about this lie as immense as a mountain.

Paul smiled broadly, satisfied with his little effect. "At Gadgetta, we love pushing the boundaries of innovation. We prioritize creativity and boldness," he explained with a series of precise, sharp gestures, squinting at times as if he were sculpting a statue with meticulous care.

She nodded, "That's fascinating. It means that..."

"Yes, I have it with me," Paul replied confidently, as if he was about to show it to her and demonstrate it.

"It's a real lighthouse!" she smiled, feeling an unexpected – and inexplicable – excitement rising within her.

Olivia burst back into the office, arms loaded with towels to wipe up the coffee stains. She was prepared. However, she was trying to hammer a nail with a tank. Seeing the long cleaning session that was about to take place, Paul changed his mind and suggested Sara change clothes. He promised he would have her stained clothes cleaned and that she could pick them up at the end of the day.

"Really, don't worry about it. It's not necessary," she said, thanking Paul and Olivia for their concern.

"No, no. You are not going to spend the whole day in stained clothes. I'm going to ask our maintenance team to take care of it immediately," Paul insisted, determined to make the situation less awkward for his new colleague.

Olivia added with a smile, "He's right. It's the least we can do. And it's our fault after all," she said as if forming a couple with Paul.

She looked at Paul. His charming smile and intense gaze seemed to say he wasn't joking.

"Well, if you really insist, thank you very much. You both are really sweet," she said, accepting the offer.

Olivia went back to her station, loaded with towels, and Paul closed his office door after pausing briefly. Then he turned around as if he was about to pull something out of a hat.

He walked a few steps in front of the large screen at the center of the room, as if he was going to present her with a magic trick, and pressed the button on the wall. Instantly, the section of the wall where the screen was mounted slid back and then to the left, revealing a hidden room.

"Here's my personal dressing room. Just help yourself. I'll make sure to get your stained clothes cleaned afterward," Paul explained with an abundance of gestures, very pleased with his little effect.

"That's really kind of you. I wasn't expecting this. It's incredible!" she said in front of this unexpected and so glamorous room.

She gazed at the dressing room greedily. It was filled with neatly arranged clothes, in matching and gradient colors. It was a real mini-boutique. The lighting presented everything beautifully. A variety of styles, both casual and formal, would allow her to easily find another outfit for the day. She had never seen anything like it. It felt a bit suspect. It even stank.

"It's the least we can do after that little incident. And besides, we're a team here, right? We help each other out," Paul added sincerely.

"Great! Thanks again."

HER FRIENDS

"I'll leave you to it. Press the button to close the door. Once you're done, it's the same button to open it. Choose whatever you like. Obviously, it's all in my size," Paul added playfully, but with genuine kindness.

"I expected as much. But that's okay. That's really nice of you, Paul," she thanked him, meeting his gaze as the dressing room door closed behind her.

Paul waited for the door to be completely shut, then jumped onto his phone, swallowing back the growing saliva.

He tapped furiously on the screen before pulling up the surveillance video from the dressing room.

He hurriedly settled into his chair, not taking his eyes off the screen, and watched with delight the image of Sara who had just removed her jacket and pants, browsing through the available styles.

Olivia opened the office door and popped her head in to inform Paul that his first appointment had arrived and was waiting at reception.

"Ah, thanks, Olivia," he replied absentmindedly, with a vacant stare and a dismissive wave, annoyed to be interrupted.

Not wanting to linger, Olivia went back, closing the door behind her.

When Paul's eyes returned to his phone screen, he found Sara was no longer there.

She had vanished from the dressing room.

"Damn... Where is she?" he muttered to himself, his heart racing in his chest.

He restarted the app several times, fearing a glitch. But the image showed an empty dressing room. He placed his phone on the desk and approached the wall where the large screen was. He held his breath, straining to catch any sound behind the sliding door. His hands trembled slightly. Then, feverishly, he turned back to his phone to check the screen again.

"Wow..." he whispered, overwhelmed, trying to calm his nerves and frustration. For a moment, he felt as if he had dreamed. "Is everything okay?" he asked in a high-pitched, worried voice.

No response came back to him. Intrigued and growing increasingly anxious, he tried once more to reach Sara, aiming to reassure himself. "Is everything going as you want?"

She was no longer visible on the surveillance video and was not answering.

He approached the opening button on the wall and pressed it. The door slid open silently, as usual, letting the sunlight flood back into the dressing room. He stepped into the small room, dumbfounded. The stained pants and jacket lay there, perfectly aligned, but there was no sign of the young woman. He genuinely wondered if he was dreaming, especially since he often found himself daydreaming. In front of this inexplicable absence, he was hit by a dizzying sensation, that feeling of losing control over reality, as if a crucial moment had just evaporated without a trace. He closed his eyes to recall the sequence of events, desperately trying to understand how she could have vanished so quickly.

He rummaged through every corner of the dressing room, moving every piece of clothing with large gestures, futilely opening drawers with growing panic, but he found no trace of her. Where the hell was she?

Disoriented, he rushed out of his office and quickly made his way to reception, where he came face to face with Olivia and Maxime, his best client.

"Ah, Maxime! Hello! Uh, excuse me, my friend, I'll be with you in a minute. I have an emergency. An unforeseen issue!" he stammered, shaking Maxime's hand, who was signaling him he was in a hurry.

Paul stepped closer to Olivia in private, looking tense, and whispered in her ear. "I've lost Sara!"

HER FRIENDS

Olivia raised her eyebrows at this unexpected declaration, sensing the extra tension surrounding Paul. "Lost? Lost?" she whispered, feeling herself pulled into his anxiety.

"She's no longer in the office!" Paul explained, a nervous freefall. Maxime was watching with curiosity, wondering what could have happened to put him in such a state.

"She's no longer in the office..." Olivia mechanically repeated to give herself time to process. "But what were you doing in the office for her to disappear like that?" she asked teasingly, trying to get him to reveal what he wanted to hide.

"Don't complicate things this morning, Olivia. She's disappeared, I tell you! Vanished. She's not here, physically!" Paul added, his tone increasingly tense, as if waiting for Olivia to give him an explanation.

Incredulous, she frowned. Then she invited Paul to follow her back to the office to unravel the mystery of the day with this sudden disappearance. She knew he sometimes needed a mother figure on hand. And that mother was her.

Their synchronized pace quickly took them to the door of the office. Olivia shot a curious glance at Paul before opening the door with a swift gesture: "I hope you haven't taken any stuff this morning, huh?"

Olivia discovered Sara standing in front of the large office table, wearing one of Paul's dark suits, having rolled up the sleeves to fit her much smaller frame. This sight was both comical and surprising, and Olivia couldn't help but burst out laughing at this unusual scene.

She looked back and forth between Paul and Sara, like watching a tennis match, with a hint of annoyance.

"Well, can you explain to me what's going on here?" she asked, wanting a clear and straightforward answer.

They finally entered the office, the tension starting to dissipate. Paul, relieved and glad to have found her safe and sound, approached her with a mix of relief and amusement. "But where have you been?"

he asked, concerned about what could have happened to their new colleague.

Sara, clearly amused by the situation, turned to Olivia and gave her a conspiratorial wink. "Don't you think it suits me perfectly?" she said, flapping her arms to emphasize how oversized the costume was compared to her frame.

Paul's relief mixed with a smirk, recognizing the mischief. Olivia, for her part, let out an exasperated sigh. "You could have warned me before raising my blood pressure," she joked, pleased to see that everything had returned to normal.

"He showed you his secret item then?" Olivia commented, "He's so proud of it!"

"Yes. In the end, I think I'll keep this costume. I actually like it!" Sara exclaimed, sliding her hands into the pockets of her pants and expanding them like a clown.

"Well, now that the mystery is solved, can we get back to work?" suggested Olivia, as she returned to her desk, amused by the antics.

Paul waited a few seconds, standing still.

"No kidding, where have you been?" he finally asked, closing the office door behind him.

She allowed herself a mischievous smile at the perfection of her ruse. She stepped confidently towards him and delicately grasped the lapel of his jacket. "You think I didn't notice your little hidden cameras? Little pervert!" she whispered playfully, mimicking a masturbation gesture.

Paul felt a jolt of electricity run through his body from head to toe, leaving him both hot and cold. He found himself trapped, and the worry on his face had given way to fear.

"It's for security protocols. We have to film. No one sees them, except in case of an incident," he retorted, trying to play innocent.

She raised an eyebrow, feigning indignation. "Oh, come on, spare me. Those haughty, disdainful excuses are for your little submissives.

HER FRIENDS

You know exactly what I'm talking about. Want me to count the fingerprints on your phone screen?" she added, twisting the knife with satisfaction.

Paul felt vulnerable in front of this teasing and cunning young woman who had just exposed his little game.

The veil of his confident boss persona was dissipating before his eyes, revealing an unexpectedly fragility he wasn't used to displaying. He was disarmed, caught off guard by this colleague who wielded wit like a master, and far more than he had anticipated.

She finally released her grip on his jacket, sending a shiver of excitement down Paul's spine. She turned away from him with a smirk, clearly enjoying the effect she had on him.

"But where were you?" Paul asked, eager to understand, "I looked everywhere!"

"No. You didn't check the ceiling," she replied, raising her finger. Paul was like the monkey who stares at the finger while being shown the moon: he was looking at the finger. And that wasn't a good sign.

"You should never underestimate the new recruits," she said, looking him straight in the eye, defying any implicit authority, "Especially when they're into climbing!"

"Wait, you were on the ceiling? What were you hanging onto?" stammered Paul, trying to imagine where she could have found a grip.

"Don't try to understand, you'll give yourself a brain strain. Where you see only walls, I see a passage. Where you see the impossible, I see an opportunity! Where there are cameras in a dressing room, there's a pervert behind them. You little scoundrel!" she exclaimed with delight.

He went back to the dressing room to check the ceiling: "Honestly, there's nothing to grab onto!" he said, incredulous and a little tense about receiving lessons first thing in the morning.

"Don't change the subject. Tell me, is that your thing? Hiring pretty girls to ogle them behind the cameras? Do you get off on the footage, is that it? Do you shake your little frustrated thing in the corner? Or worse, do you post them online to amuse your friends and earn their respect? Is that your sick fantasy?" she reproached him.

Paul put on a fascinating show. His face changed through every color of emotion, going from white to pink, then from pink to purple, short of breath, all in plain sight.

"You know, let's leave it at that because you're sweet. But I've had my fill of sickos like you," she said in a frosty tone, her voice trembling with pent-up anger.

He looked at her, disarmed, and hurriedly followed her to the door.

"Don't go. That was very clumsy of me, I admit," he said gravely, trying to apologize.

She looked at him as if she had just discovered a different man. Paul's words no longer unsettled her at all.

"You'll have my belongings delivered. You've damaged them. Maybe deliberately? Thanks!"

"I'm confused, I..."

"And above all, destroy those images. Don't try to spy on me at home. I'm going to file a police report immediately," she thundered, pushing Paul's hand away when he tried to stop her.

She left the office with determination. She left Paul stunned. He wasn't accustomed to being exposed, and clearly even less accustomed to being given orders.

She strode down the hallway to the reception desk, leaning in to Olivia's ear: "I'm leaving. You could have warned me!"

"Wait! Where are you going?" Olivia asked, a distressed pout on her face, not understanding.

"I'm leaving it to you, darling!" Sara replied, mimicking the gesture of tossing a tissue into a bin, then turning around to press the elevator call button.

HER FRIENDS

Carpooling

Justine's Car

"Can I drop you off here?" Justine asked her colleague Melinda as the sun slowly set on the horizon, bathing the city in golden light after a long day of work.

Melinda, touched by this gesture, turned her gaze toward Justine with sincere gratitude. "Yes, thank you from the bottom of my heart, Justine. You are incredibly generous to accompany me every evening like this."

A warm smile lit up Justine's face as she simply replied, "It's on my way, Melinda, and I enjoy our conversations. They brighten my day, you know."

The streets were bathed in a soft glow, and the two friends continued their conversation as urban life buzzed around them. Their shared laughter echoed in the car, while they exchanged office anecdotes and well-kept secrets.

"Oh, don't downplay what you're doing, Justine. We all go through tough times, but I can't help but think about that terrifying dream you had where you were kidnapped in a car. It was incredibly stressful. Let it go, Justine. I really hope you don't have nightmares like that anymore."

Melinda got out of the car, giving a wave and offering a compassionate smile. Their eyes met for a moment, reflecting the bond that had developed between them.

Justine reciprocated the gesture and then continued her journey along the avenue on that bright day. Deep down, she still felt unsettled and troubled, desperately seeking the comfort she lacked. The city stretched out around her, yet her mind remained trapped in that car where terror had embraced her, where two sinister men had confronted

HER FRIENDS

her with horror. She tried to think of something else, but the images from that car were haunting and quickly took over again.

PAUL TOSKIAM

The Doctors

The Martian Institute's 4x4 vehicle

In the elevator, Sara was furious.
　The image of that detestable Paul haunted her. What a jerk, just good for harassing women in his office! What vermin! Thankfully, she had managed to escape his manipulation. You never know how far these perverts can go.
　As she was heading towards the building's exit, lost in her thoughts, her phone, which kept vibrating, rang once more.
　"What? No, I didn't order a taxi. Have a good day," she said tersely before hanging up. She really didn't have time for sales calls; in fact, it was never a good time.
　Once outside, she found herself face to face with a large, black car parked right in front of the building's entrance. It was the kind of car that transported stars and important people. A blond man stood in front of it, and as he saw her approaching, he opened the back door on the sidewalk side. He appeared to mock her with his suit that was far too big. Thinking the car was meant for someone else, she decided to continue walking down the sidewalk. But she was quickly intercepted by a taller, dark-haired man.
　"Sara Blisken?" asked the dark-haired man, holding her arm to stop her.
　"Yes?" she replied.
　"Your car is ready," he said.
　"But I didn't order a car. Were you the one who just called me? There must be a mistake," she retorted, freeing her arm and continuing her walk.

"Get in the car. Don't make a fuss," he ordered in a tone that left her no choice, grabbing her arm again.

"What are you doing? Let go of me right now!" she shouted, annoyed.

Panic set in as she took out her phone and dialed the emergency number to call the police. The dark-haired man snatched the device from her in a quick, precise movement.

"There's no way out!" he said with no expression on his face, as if he did this all day.

"How do you know my name? Are you the police?" she asked, trying to understand why the police would want to take her in if she wanted to report the unacceptable behavior she had just suffered.

The dark-haired man didn't answer. He simply pointed to the black car with his hand, as if it were the only possible destination. Panic-stricken, she began to scream and struggle instinctively, but she quickly lost control of the situation. She stared with great curiosity at his hand on her arm, feeling no desire to scream or run away anymore. She felt good, relaxed. It was a pleasant, enveloping feeling, something almost orgasmic.

Without needing further encouragement, she took a few steps toward the car and settled across from the two men in the back. The interior resembled a small lounge with a table in the middle.

"Thank you, gentlemen... I appreciate your kindness... It's so rare these days," she thanked them with a drunken smile.

The dark-haired man indicated for her to buckle her seatbelt, and she complied gladly.

"Here, drink this," he said, handing her a glass as the vehicle started moving.

"Okay," she replied cheerfully. "Um... this is delicious; what is it?"

"The antidote," he explained in a neutral tone before taking the glass back and placing it in the small bar beside him.

"What is it?" she murmured, feeling dizzy.

HER FRIENDS

"It will pass in a few seconds," he said to reassure her, gazing thoughtfully at the traffic.

Indeed, a few seconds later, she perceived the world through the eyes of someone who has just woken up after a good night's sleep. She stared at the two men in front of her and the car's interior. It looked like a limousine for raucous nights out with friends, with lights and speakers everywhere. Strangers, a car, drugs... She thought that maybe this is how dozens of people disappeared without a trace. In any case, she was still alive and intended to stay that way.

"What am I doing in this car, exactly? Who are you?" she asked.

The two men continued to gaze out at the passing urban landscape without saying a word.

"Hey! I'm talking to you! What am I doing in this car? And who are you, damn it!"

No response.

"Please park by the sidewalk; I'm getting out!" she demanded, turning to the driver only to realize there was no driver.

"Okay. Shall we introduce ourselves? Nice to meet you, I'm Sara Blisken. What's going on here?"

Still no response.

Faced with these two silent strangers, a small voice inside her told her not to linger in that car. Getting away as quickly as possible wasn't the simplest option, but probably the safest. That morning was already packed with emotions and was starting to become overwhelming. She scanned for a projectile, her eyes bouncing nervously around. Her bag could do, but there wasn't much inside to knock out two healthy guys. Her eyes finally landed on a briefcase carelessly placed on the side of the mini-lounge. "Funny how you don't notice things until you need them!" she thought, almost salivating at the thought of this suitcase becoming an unexpected weapon. It was one of those silver metal models and looked exactly like something that could sufficiently harm the two cold statues. The plan was to strike hard enough to knock them out, then open the door and jump out of the vehicle. She knew it was akin to jumping from a balcony when the apartment was on fire, but her imagination and rising stress provided her with no other option that morning. She inwardly laughed, picturing herself as an action hero. Did it really hurt to jump from a moving car, even at low speed?

"Don't even think about it," the dark-haired man warned immediately, his eyes following her movements carefully.

"Oh, you're alive!" she exclaimed, relieved at the unexpected return of her interlocutor to some form of humanity. Little details are reassuring when you're scared.

They exchanged furtive glances, each trying to anticipate the other's intentions, like in a Western duel. They all knew the situation was about to explode, but neither man seemed ready to make the first move. Guided by her instincts, she suddenly grabbed the briefcase with both hands. She lifted it above her head, inadvertently scraping the entire ceiling, and threw it with all her might at the two men in a cry of liberating rage. The intense vibrations from her vocal cords even gave her a boost of confidence. Without wasting any time, she unbuckled her seatbelt and dove over the table to continue hitting the two men, appearing intent on reducing them to dust. She held tightly to the briefcase she had caught in front of her face and couldn't see what was happening behind her. The fight raged on, neither of them easily giving in. She screamed and hit with all her might and weight. But her opponents were skilled as well. The briefcase violently hit Sara's face, sending her crashing backward in the process. She found herself sprawled back in her original position, her legs splayed on the table like at the gynecologist's, half-stunned. She had rarely taken such a hard suitcase blow to the face. In her quiet little life, guys usually let her dominate. But these two certainly seemed like new specimens to add to her collection of brutality.

As she attempted to rise, touching her pained face, the blond man leaned over the table to help her sit up and fastened her seatbelt.

HER FRIENDS

Meanwhile, the dark-haired man spoke into his watch. She couldn't understand everything, but he mentioned a target, a departure, and a briefing. It was certain; with this kind of hit to the face and the burning pain she felt: she had a broken nose.

She felt droplets flow down to her mouth, tasting her blood. The blond who had joined her beside her pulled out a small first-aid kit from a side cabinet and offered to tend to her nose. At first, she refused to let this stranger touch her, but when he showed her reflection in a small square mirror, she accepted.

"Oh my God, my nose!" she gasped, almost speaking to herself, disappointed and shocked to discover this red mess in the middle of her face.

"Let me introduce myself; I'm Dr. Carlo Mancini," the dark-haired man said with a wide smile.

"Alright, alright. But can you please drop me off by the sidewalk? I promise I won't say anything to the police," she asked through gritted teeth from the pain.

"And I'm Dr. Lucas Fischer, nice to meet you," the blond introduced himself, nodding his head. "Try to stay still. I'm going to disinfect," he continued, beginning to dab the blood off Sara's face.

"I'm sorry for these circumstances, but you've been chosen to participate in a special mission," Carlo declared in a calm voice.

She frowned, her nose pain almost forgotten for a moment. "A special mission? You mean for the secret services?"

He shook his head. "No, nothing like that. This is a completely different matter. We've discovered an imminent threat of extraterrestrials approaching Earth. We've developed a powerful weapon to block them, but it requires a specific fuel."

She feigned surprise at this story that was starting to sound like a joke.

"Honestly, I've had my share of ridiculous events this morning. Don't you have anything else?" she sighed, grimacing.

"I pressed too hard; I'm sorry," Lucas apologized, "Try to move less."

"I know, saying it like that... is the sad reality. Initially, we detected an asteroid. A big one, over ten kilometers in diameter. Its signature was completely ordinary. The size was significant, but the trajectory posed no problems. Then two weeks ago, it inexplicably and artificially deviated," Carlo explained pensively.

"Honestly, doctor... doctor of what, anyway?" she asked, curious.

"Lucas and I are surgeons."

"Oh, right... So, you kidnapped me and broke my nose to charge me for a cosmetic procedure? Honestly, an email would have sufficed. I wouldn't have read it, that's true!"

"For the nose, I'm sorry, but you didn't leave us many options..." Carlo said, smiling mischievously. He pointed to the scar that one of the suitcase corners had just given him above his left eyebrow. "We need you," he added.

"Need me? For what?" she wondered. Even in the most unlikely situations, she tended to find likable people who showed interest in her. She hated this bias in others. And she hated it even more in herself. Especially at this moment in her life, so fraught with uncertainties and a lack of self-confidence. So, any interest that could be found in her made her naively happy—even if just for a few seconds.

"You are the key, Sara," Lucas whispered in her ear.

"What? Look, I'm not a scientist," she exclaimed. "How can a poor unemployed purchasing manager be of any use in your asteroid story? And you two tell me, you seem to know me well anyway, right?" Carlo looked at her, nodding his head, amused. "No, really, I'm telling you, you'd better pull over and drop me off on the sidewalk. I'm going to slow you down unnecessarily; I can feel it."

"You're funny!" Lucas commented.

"It's fine, I'll manage to get home, don't worry. And I won't tell the police, I promise!" she explained while trying to evade Lucas's delicate gestures on her nose.

HER FRIENDS

"I'm really angry this morning. I mean, before I met you, I encountered a kind of jerk I almost worked with. It drove me crazy. I probably overreacted, but it was visceral, beyond my control. And on top of that, you show up with your ridiculous stories!"

"That's exactly what we need: for you to be really angry."

"Oh yeah? You want my fist in your face?"

"I suggest something else. You only have one nose, and it's in bad shape," Carlo commented with a discreet chuckle.

"We needed your DNA to be stressed, in a way. It's in this exact configuration that we need to collect it, in less than an hour now; otherwise, it will have returned to its initial state, and we will have to start all over again. You should be just right," Lucas added, very sure of himself.

"What tact, Dr. Gunter! You're talking about me like I'm just a piece of meat. I'm your little obedient guinea pig. Is that your plan?" she asserted, astounded.

The two men exchanged another furtive glance, and Lucas calmly replied, "Yes."

A silence settled in the vehicle. Each one observed the other without speaking. The tipping point had been reached for Sara.

"By the way, my last name is Fischer, Lucas Fischer. And stop looking at me with those accusing eyes. I'm not going to eat you. It's just a blood draw."

"Oh, don't be so touchy, Dr. Muller. I'm the one being deprived of my freedom right now!" Sara yelled to set things straight.

"Stop! We have better things to do than squabble. We'll be there soon. Sara, you're going to be taken care of for the blood draw. We're going to give you a new nose..." Carlo explained.

"Finally! I've always wanted to get rid of this ugly bump; it gives me a vulture profile," she said, mimicking a bump in the air and pointing at her nose.

"You understood me. We're going to fix your nose properly," Carlo clarified kindly, noticing that Sara was starting, perhaps even without realizing it, to collaborate with them.

"Is the blood draw mandatory? I don't like needles. You can take a bit of saliva, you know?" she suggested with a bitter expression on her face, as if she had just swallowed something particularly unpleasant.

"We need a complete genetic assessment," Lucas explained without acknowledging Sara's humor.

"Well, tell me, Dr. Bellini, your friend doesn't seem very relaxed," Sara pointed out.

"Mancini. Carlo Mancini. We're in a very complicated situation. I hope you understand that now. Do you understand?" he asked, waiting impatiently for a response.

"Yes. After all, otherwise, you wouldn't have treated my nose so well, would you? Unless... Anyway, thank you for your care," she said, wondering why she was thanking them, and giving Lucas a smile that was meant to be grateful.

Looking out the window, she realized she didn't know this area.

"Where are we?" she asked, anxious.

"I can't tell you right now. You'll find out soon. We'll arrive in five minutes," Carlo indicated.

"Can I have my phone? I'd like to let my father know. We planned to have lunch together," Sara attempted, assuming she wouldn't be getting her phone back anytime soon.

"Yes, of course. Here it is," Carlo said, handing her the device.

Surprised, she looked at him for a long time, trying to understand where the trap was.

"Go ahead, Sara, you can use it. Don't look at me like that: there's no trap," he laughed.

"So I can call whoever I want and say whatever I want?" she asked, still taken aback.

HER FRIENDS

"Yes, go ahead. You have my full trust. From now on, you are an integral part of our team, Sara. You have a new job. And anyway, who would believe you?" Carlo exclaimed, bursting into contagious laughter, quickly followed by the other two.

PAUL TOSKIAM

The Car Descent

The Martian Institute's premises

Dr. Mancini, a young man around her age, was dressed casually in a simple white shirt, jeans, and barely laced sneakers. From the very first glance, she had noticed the undeniable charisma that radiated from him. He spoke in a calm voice, oscillating between deep and high notes, which gave him the range of a lyrical singer. Every time he dropped to a lower note on a syllable, it had an indescribable effect on Sara, who was particularly sensitive to such nuances. His gestures exuded ease and grace, while his smile lit up his entire face, giving him an instant air of serenity. It was clear that this man had a talent for seduction, and he was surely aware of it. Yet, he wasn't playing with it, which made his allure even more captivating. Perhaps the situation didn't call for it, or maybe he simply wasn't "hungry," in the figurative sense, of course. This was a common phenomenon among attractive people: they draw others to them like magnets. And right now, Sara was easily drawn to anything resembling a handsome guy. She knew she was ready for a love story. She simply needed it.

    She glanced at her phone. She wanted to call her father to apologize for missing their planned lunch together. But she was too tense to engage in a conversation, even a short one. She dreaded the "but why?", the "is everything okay?", the "how is your first day at work going otherwise?" and all those little things that an adorable dad like hers loved to know about his only daughter. Jane composed a message, corrected it several times, and added a few hearts, promising to call him later. She stared at the message for a few seconds, her mind blank, before pressing the send button. She remained lost in thought for a moment longer. It was that damned feeling of guilt that rushed back. It had never truly dissipated since her father was diagnosed and operated on for prostate cancer last year.

George responded sooner than expected and in an unexpected way: "Sara, a monster has come to pick you up at home. I'm at the police station."

She fixed her two travel companions with a pensive look.

"Is everything okay?" Carlo asked, visibly worried by her prolonged silence.

"I... I don't know. I need to call my father," she said in a trembling voice.

Carlo waved her on, signaling that she could go ahead and call.

"SARA, YOU ARE IN DANGER," came the message from Mobo. She didn't know any "Mobo." What was that doing in her contacts? These spam messages had reached an alarming level of sophistication.

She lifted her head and met his gaze, unable to look away. It was as if he was reading her thoughts, that little brat.

"It's okay. I'm all yours. We'll be there, I think!" she said spontaneously.

"Yes. Do you know the area?"

"No, I'm joking. I've never been around here. Warehouses aren't really my thing."

"You'll see, ours is special," Carlo boasted, his eyes sparkling as if he were talking about a cave filled with priceless treasure.

"Here, put this on," Lucas offered, handing her a badge to wear as a necklace. "This will save you from having to explain yourself if you get lost."

She turned to him, doubly surprised: "Is it that big? And where did you get that photo from? I've never worn that kind of bimbo hairstyle!"

"Sorry, we had to do it quickly. It's a generated image. It still resembles you quite a bit, doesn't it?" he explained, amused, gesturing around her face.

HER FRIENDS

"Can you tell me how you know so much about me?" she asked, looking at Carlo.

"Don't worry. We'll meet up in a little less than an hour now. We're catching a flight to Cairo. I'll explain everything then."

"Oh no. I just got back from vacation. I don't want to leave again!" she joked half-heartedly.

"Your father can come with you if you want," Lucas suggested.

Surprised, she paused, lost in thought without saying anything.

"Thank you for offering. He's too weak for the adventure," she said, her gaze still on the horizon.

And that horizon was the small entrance to a massive hangar in front of which the vehicle had just stopped.

"Damn, what are all those armed guys? And those sunglasses? Are you expecting a star or something?" Sara exclaimed, pointing at a dozen men in black sunglasses, armed to the teeth.

"The star has arrived, and she's about to get out of the car in a few seconds," Lucas revealed, amused.

She exchanged glances with the two men, who were gently teasing her for not getting it herself. They were engrossed in their mobile screens, closely observing the surroundings as if they were searching for something specific.

"Come on, you two, that's enough! Do you really think I'm stupid? I haven't been working for anti-alien services for over ten years!" she retorted, slightly frustrated but also amused by their attitude.

"Sara, the car is going to stop right in front of that big gate. Do you see it?" Carlo pointed out. "We'll open the gate, then you'll get out of the car crouched, please, and you'll run straight toward that gate without stopping. Is that clear?" he asked to ensure she would spend as little time as possible in the open air.

She alternated her gaze between the gate, the armed men, and Carlo. If there was something she needed to understand about all this protocol reserved for her, it was that her life was in danger. And she understood that at that precise moment. She processed that distressing idea both mentally and physically.

"You will have to be brave, Sara," Carlo continued, "You absolutely must stay alive for the next five days. Well, I mean, five days and more, of course," he added, embarrassed by his clumsiness.

"Listen, I don't understand everything, but yes, okay. Shall I go?" she asked, pointing at the door that had just opened.

"No! Wait a few more seconds," Carlo asked as Lucas descended from the vehicle first, heading toward the gate with two metal suitcases in hand.

"Now!" Carlo whispered, nudging Sara toward the exit as if she were about to sky dive.

She fixed her eyes on the gate and began her crouched run as instructed, not daring to look away. Yet suddenly, she turned back and stood up.

"Damn, I forgot my bag!" she muttered as she went back to the car, just before taking a bullet to the neck and falling backward onto the ground.

"SARA!" Carlo screamed from the car.

Immediately, he ordered the guards to retrieve Sara's bleeding body and transport it inside while a hail of crossfire descended upon them.

Half of the guards were killed on the spot, but the others, despite their multiple injuries, managed to carry Sara inside the gate. She had lost consciousness.

Lucas dropped his suitcases and rushed over to help her. At the same time, he called for emergency services while speaking into his watch. A full team of medics arrived within seconds, and Sara was rushed directly into an operating room.

Breathless and shocked, Lucas gave rapid instructions with swift gestures to Carlo, who exited the car and dashed crouched toward the gate. Once inside the building, he stood up and stayed there, frozen,

HER FRIENDS

watching the stretcher get further away, leaving a trail of a few drops of blood on the ground behind him.

"We should have gone around the back and entered the car," he muttered, as Lucas shot him a piercing look, betraying the obvious fact that it wouldn't have made much difference.

The Martian

The Martian Institute's premises

"What have you done? What happened?" Kurtz Schwartz erupted, violently pounding his fists on his desk as if he wanted to smash it to pieces. "Seriously, what have you done, you bunch of incompetents?" he continued, standing up and pacing the room.

Carlo and Lucas sat stoically in the chairs before the desk, holding their breath and observing Kurtz's movements like two kittens.

Kurtz abruptly stopped in front of Carlo and Lucas, glaring at them with anger. "I simply cannot believe you let this happen!" he thundered. "Sara has been injured due to your negligence and your inability to carry out your mission properly. You have failed, you bunch of incompetents!"

Carlo looked up at Kurtz, remaining calm despite the intensity of the situation. "Kurtz, we understand your frustration, but we took every necessary precaution. We couldn't have foreseen this situation."

Kurtz stepped closer to Carlo, pointing an accusatory finger at him. "You could have and you should have!" he retorted. "You are responsible for the team's safety, and you have failed in that duty. Now, Sara is injured, and our mission is compromised."

Lucas intervened, trying to calm the tumultuous atmosphere. "Kurtz, we all agree to take responsibility for our mistakes..."

"Lucas, I didn't create this institute to lose a vital target just hours before a major confrontation. Is that clear in your little head?" Kurtz growled, his teeth clenched just like his fists. Kurtz was hot-blooded, always ready to argue forcefully.

HER FRIENDS

"Kurtz, this was bound to happen; we planned this extraction at the last minute. We had no time to reassess the situation..." Lucas tried to explain.

"Stop! Don't talk to me about fatalism or amateurism! Where is she right now?" Kurtz demanded, his gaze fixed on Lucas.

"She is in the operating room and receiving the best medical care we can provide. She will get the best possible treatment."

Kurtz stepped back slightly, regaining his composure. He knew Lucas was right, but that did nothing to lessen his anger and disappointment. "Very well," he sighed. "But if she doesn't survive, you're out. And don't think I will forget this negligence. We need to learn from this situation and ensure it doesn't happen again in the future."

Carlo and Lucas nodded silently, fully aware of the gravity of the situation. They knew they would need to make amends and work harder to regain Kurtz's trust.

"You are absolutely right," Carlo said as he stood up. "This is entirely my fault. I should have kept her sedated until we reached the destination, as planned. I changed the protocol, and that was an unforgivable mistake," he continued. Lucas stared at him, as if Carlo had just announced that the Earth was flat.

"My dear Carlo, I like you, you know that? Just as I appreciated your poor father, may he rest in peace. But please, stop your childish antics. I don't expect you to suck up to me. We knew they could shoot from afar. We didn't know they could shoot from that far, and with such precision. None of us could have imagined it, let alone foresee it. Now, I need you to carry this mission to total success, because I am paying you for that. And I have complete confidence in both of you. Is that clear?" Kurtz explained, gesturing that the conversation was over and that they could leave.

The two doctors wondered how they would cope with this pressure, outside of their usual responsibilities and expertise. Kurtz was no stranger to contradictions.

He had taken the helm of the Martian, an institute focused on space development, alongside his wife, Bertha. It was back when they met in Ibiza. They were young and carefree, dreaming of the stars and wanting to experience them. So they joined this institute for research and exploration founded in the distant past. The greatest minds in history had at one point or another worked with the Martian. They transformed it into what it is today: the only bulwark capable of countering an attack.

After his wife's death, Kurtz completely changed. He became a patriarch, someone who had seen and experienced everything, with a raw and binary foundation, yet a benevolent surface. Like all binary profiles, this is what made him formidable to his contemporaries. He knew how to wield fire and ice. He had the ability to turn your guts inside out with just a few words. He was someone you both hated and admired in equal measure.

Carlo had been recruited into the institute by his own father. And he had in turn recruited Lucas, one of his best friends from university.

HER FRIENDS

The Fate of Struiz

Flagship

Admiral Struiz was urgently summoned to the grand audience chamber, feeling his unease grow since he had received the news.

He was struck by a terrible discomfort in his bathroom, and the signs of his misfortune were visible everywhere. He had unknowingly redecorated the room, under the influence of violent spasms, repainting almost all the surfaces with vomit: the floor, the walls, the ceiling. Ruminating on this unexpected summons, he realized that it could not be a coincidence. Worse still, he did not know how to redeem himself in front of his superior, the Grand Master.

He, who had the reputation of never missing his target, now found himself having to justify his actions.

The grand audience chamber was immersed in semi-darkness. Only a faint light coming from the enormous bay window illuminated the room slightly. Admiral Struiz was once again immediately seized by the oppressive silence that reigned in these solemn halls. He could not get used to such grandeur. The walls were adorned with historical frescoes featuring stern characters. They seemed to stare him down, judging him with a hostile intensity.

In the center of the room, a large dark wood table majestically dominated, surrounded by leather chairs occupied by members of the council. Struiz could feel the cold sweat bead along his forehead as his imagination envisioned all sorts of disastrous scenarios.

His unease grew with every step he took. The murmurs of the guards stationed at the entrance faded slowly as Struiz approached the table. He tried in vain to calm the frantic beating of his heart, but fear crept into every corner of his being.

HER FRIENDS

Finally, he reached the table, standing there before the Grand Master and the other council members. Struiz could not help but notice their severe and impenetrable expressions, further amplifying his discomfort. The Grand Master, dressed in a long purple cloak, fixed him with a cold gaze.

"Admiral Struiz, sit down," the Grand Master solemnly commanded, motioning to a seat beside him.

Struiz complied, feeling every inch of his skin tingle as he sank into the leather chair. The council members said nothing, observing the admiral with gazes that seemed to penetrate deep into his soul.

"Admiral Struiz, you are here for a serious reason," the Grand Master began in a cutting voice. "You missed your target during the mission that was assigned to you. Can you explain this?"

Struiz felt his heart skip a beat. He knew this question would be asked. Yet, it seemed insurmountable to find a satisfactory answer. He tried to gather his thoughts, to organize the chaotic memories that assaulted him.

"Your Excellency, I have no valid excuse," he replied in a broken voice. "I did everything to reach my target, but..."

"But?" interjected the Grand Master sharply. "There is no 'but' in a mission as crucial as this one. You were our best asset, our spearhead, and you have failed."

The Grand Master's voice echoed in the chamber, amplified by a sinister echo. Struiz lowered his head, feeling overwhelmed by the weight of his own failure. He could not believe he had betrayed the trust placed in him and began to vomit violently, splattering part of the council table and splashing a few members.

"Master, rest assured that..." he began in a trembling voice.

"Silence!" interrupted the Grand Master with undeniable authority. "We have no regard for your excuses. What we want is an explanation. How could you miss your target?"

The question resonated in Struiz's mind as he wiped his mouth with his sleeve, desperately searching for a plausible answer. His gaze drifted involuntarily to the wall frescoes that seemed to mock him. He then remembered the discomfort he had felt in his bathroom and instinctively understood that it was related to his failure.

"Your Excellency, I do not know how to explain it," he admitted quietly. "Before the mission, I was struck by a violent malaise. Then just moments ago in my bathroom. I was unable to control myself, and the consequences are now visible before you," he explained, gesturing toward the sullied table.

The council members exchanged puzzled glances, while the Grand Master remained impassive. Struiz felt as though he were being judged, subjected to silent inquiries that penetrated deep within him.

"Admiral Struiz, are you implying that your sudden illness caused your failure during the mission?" the Grand Master asked in a dry voice.

Struiz knew this explanation was implausible and of poor quality. But he had nothing to lose now. He decided to reveal everything, to lay himself bare before the council.

"I understand this may sound absurd, Your Excellency, but I cannot deny the facts," Struiz began with a resolute voice. "I suffered from violent spasms. I have been vomiting since then. I simply could not control myself. I did manage to touch her throat. But, certainly, I did not kill her."

The council members seemed horrified, beginning to fidget in their seats, but Struiz continued unabashedly.

"I do not know how or why this happened to me. But I am convinced that it affected my abilities during the mission. I was physically weakened, and it impaired my judgment and my accuracy. I never miss, usually."

A heavy silence fell upon the chamber, each member contemplating Struiz's words. The Grand Master cast a scrutinizing gaze at the admiral, appearing to search for any flaw in his account.

HER FRIENDS

"Bring in our most esteemed doctors," the Grand Master finally ordered. "We must assess the truthfulness of your claims, Admiral. If you are lying or attempting to conceal your incompetence, the consequences could be fatal."

Struiz nodded, aware of the importance of proving his sincerity. He had hoped this explanation would suffice, but he now knew he would have to submit to extensive medical examinations. He feared for his reputation, his career, and even his life.

The doctors arrived quickly, accompanied by technicians and nurses. They conducted a series of tests on Struiz, using complex instruments to analyze his health. Then they exited, along with the Grand Master, who took this matter very seriously. Their professionalism was undeniable, but the admiral felt a twinge of anxiety. His fate was in their hands.

After a long wait, the doctors returned to the audience chamber, still accompanied by the Grand Master. The latter's expression was inscrutable, giving no hint as to the forthcoming conclusion.

"Admiral Struiz, the results of our examinations are unexpected," the Grand Master began in a neutral tone. "It appears you suffered from a severe allergic reaction to a food you recently consumed."

Struiz was stunned. An allergic reaction? He would never have imagined that this could be the cause of his discomfort. He had always believed that his failure was due to an unexplained illness or some kind of curse.

"Our doctors found that you have an intolerance to a food commonly used in our base," explained the Grand Master. "Your body reacted severely to this substance, resulting in violent spasms and your inability to complete your mission."

Struiz was speechless. A mere food intolerance had caused his downfall. He felt a mix of humiliation and relief, knowing that his failure was not entirely his fault.

"Admiral Struiz, know that we take this new information into account," the Grand Master declared with some leniency. "Your reputation speaks for itself, and your past successes compel us to consider these exceptional circumstances. However, you will have to prove yourself once again. You must prove that you are still worthy of your rank. You must kill her and bring me her DNA!"

Struiz nodded, realizing that this second chance was a rare privilege. He was determined to restore his reputation, to show the council that he was still the best in his field.

"I will not disappoint you, Grand Master. I will do everything in my power to regain my focus and restore my reputation," he promised, his voice filled with determination.

The Grand Master's gaze softened slightly, revealing a glimmer of hope.

"We trust you, Admiral," he concluded. "Stand up and prove to us that you are worthy of our trust."

Struiz rose, feeling the eyes of the council members weigh upon him. He knew that his path would be arduous, but he was ready to face the challenge. With renewed resolve, he left the grand audience chamber, determined to restore his honor and reclaim his place as the spearhead of the fleet.

HER FRIENDS

The Awakening

The Martian Institute's premises

The large room stood out with its baroque style, surprisingly mixed with the more traditional setting of the hospital. The immaculate walls, a brilliant white, were adorned with delicate moldings and intricate sculptures, reminiscent of the lavish periods in history.

At the center of the room was furniture of unparalleled elegance. A large canopied bed draped in a fabric embroidered with gold had become the focal point of this extraordinary chamber. The bed's feet had been meticulously carved, forming twisted volutes and sophisticated arabesques. The sheets, a sparkling white, were soft and silky, inviting rest and tranquility.

Not far from the bed, a chest of precious wood stood proudly, inlaid with elaborate marquetry. Floral patterns, crafted with extreme precision, intertwined on the drawers, offering a splash of color in this ocean of white. Delicate porcelain vases filled with flowers in matching colors, carefully arranged, testified to the meticulous attention paid to detail in every corner of the room.

Positioned near the bed, a battery of imposing and complex machines had kept Sara alive. The gentle mechanical sounds emanating from these sophisticated devices created a discreet yet present electronic symphony. Monitors displaying wavering curves and alarming numbers constantly tracked her vital signs. Delicate tubes emerged from her pale skin, connecting her to these life-sustaining machines.

Above the bed, a huge respirator breathed for her, regularly blowing a mist of therapeutic oxygen. Its transparent tubes coiled around the bed, echoing the volutes of the room's sculptures. Next

HER FRIENDS

to this mechanical monster, a futuristic heart monitor blinked confidently, illuminating the room intermittently with a bluish hue.

The noise of the machines resonated in the room, like a gentle symphony that had cradled Sara in her sleep. They had come to life, somewhat like the carved gargoyles on the walls, vigilantly watching over her with unwavering precision.

Sara, still asleep, lay peacefully in the midst of this hallucinatory tableau. Her pale, serene face contrasted with the complexity of the machines that had sustained her. One might almost say she was an integral part of this singular universe, like a fragile porcelain doll, surrounded by extravagant ornaments and high technology.

Yet, in this room, the fragile balance between life and death had become tangible. Every detail, every motif, and every machine seemed to narrate a story, a story in which Sara was both protagonist and victim.

A blue liquid flowed through one of the transparent tubes and entered the veins of Sara's left arm. A few minutes later, she began to move, first a little, then finally waking up.

One of the robotic arms slowly removed her oxygen mask. As soon as she began to breathe the fresh air of the room with her own lungs, a small army of caregivers burst around her bed. She tried to look at them, but her dizziness was still too intense. She attempted to sit up a little, but was immediately seized by nausea and a strong urge to vomit.

She felt weak and disoriented, unable to comprehend what was happening around her. The deafening sounds of the machines and the rapid movements of the caretakers intimidated her. She longed to ask questions, to seek explanations, but her voice refused to come out. All she could do was anxiously observe her strange surroundings and try to understand her situation.

Her vision was blurry, as if gel had been applied over her eyes. She desperately tried to remember what had led to this situation, but her memories were just as foggy, as if an opaque mist had enveloped her recent recollections. Feeling isolated and fragile, she nonetheless found herself at the heart of a bustling activity around her.

"Welcome, Sara. I'm Olivia. I will help you wake up. The operation went well. We will equip you now."

She wore a form-fitting space suit that accentuated her elegant curves. The fabric shimmered softly in the ambient light, creating a mysterious aura around her. Complex patterns in electric blue sparkled along her arms and legs, contrasting with the rest of the outfit. These glowing designs changed color gently, creating a hypnotic dance that immediately captured attention.

Organic-moving areas also dotted Olivia's body. Panels made from biocompatible materials, similar to synthetic skin, were integrated into the outfit, forming circular sections that pulsed gently like living cells. These organic areas breathed, giving the impression that the whole ensemble was alive.

The electronic parts of this suit were equipped with built-in touch controls, allowing her to control different aspects of her outfit with a mere touch.

Focusing intently, she pressed a multitude of buttons on the surrounding machines, and her voice was distant, with a short metallic echo.

In an extreme effort, Sara lifted her head to observe the young woman. "Olivia," that name triggered a series of images and recent memories.

"Olivia? What are you doing here?" Sara articulated, with a thick, robotic voice, unable to keep the saliva from dribbling down her chin. "Damn! What is this terrible voice? I sound like a toy!"

Olivia tapped a few seconds on her console and gave Sara a peaceful smile.

"Don't move yet. Don't exert yourself. I will give you one last injection, and you will regain your abilities. Stay still in the meantime." Olivia gently stroked her hair in a soothing gesture.

HER FRIENDS

Sara had flashbacks of the incident - getting out of the car, running toward the door, then the void. She remembered an intense pain in her neck, a sensation never before felt. It was excruciating, as if something had struck her neck with unimaginable force, followed by unbearable pain.

"That's it, it's over. You will regain your strength very soon. You see me better now, don't you?" Olivia asked, slightly adjusting the position of Sara's head without touching her, using a mechanized arm.

"Yes. I see you, but that's not my voice! What is this voice?"

"Something temporary. Don't worry. You have lost the use of your vocal cords. You'll be able to choose from our catalog. By the way, you can change your voice as you wish now," Olivia explained while briefly playing snippets of the countless available voices.

Sara looked at the screen, listening very intrigued, but with great interest.

"I want a slutty voice!" she exclaimed, before bursting into laughter with Olivia, who selected some options on her screen and began to speak with a "slutty" voice.

"You mean, a voice like this?" she asked.

"Damn! You have one too? Did you lose your voice?" Sara asked, pausing, astonished.

"No, I'm made this way. But I rarely change my voice. Occasionally, in the evening for fun,"

Olivia said, reverting to her original voice at the end of her sentence.

"Olivia. Thank you for taking care of me like this," said Sara, gazing at her intently.

"Oh, don't say that. We are responsible for that terrible accident. We should have protected you more. We couldn't have known," Olivia replied, her gaze lost in thought.

"You're no longer at the reception, then?"

Olivia smiled as if it were a poorly kept secret. "No, we all played a role in raising your pressure. I admit it was a bit amateurish. It was Carlo's idea. He wanted your anger to gradually grow, in stages. According to him, it depended on the quality of your DNA sample. I don't have all the details. I'm just responsible for advancing the mission," Olivia revealed calmly.

"The mission?"

"They didn't tell you? I thought your car ride had taken a while?"

"It did, but I didn't understand everything. Mostly, I didn't believe all this. Until that thing in my throat, or neck, I don't know. What happened to me?"

Olivia moved toward a large cabinet that had just been brought into the room and elegantly opened it.

"Look! Here's your eye. In fact, you only need one. You also lost the use of your left eye. We will install a synthetic eye during the flight."

"What flight?" Sara asked, sitting up completely on the bed.

"Oh, they didn't tell you?"

"No. Well, yes. I'm not sure anymore."

"You're leaving for Paris in a few minutes."

She looked at Olivia as if she had just revealed that Santa Claus wasn't real.

"Paris? What are we going to do there? Shopping?" she attempted to joke.

"No, don't worry. But I'd rather Paul explain it to you. He does it better than I do."

"Paul? Are you referring to the Paul from the cloakroom?" she exclaimed.

"Yes, that one!" Olivia replied with a laugh, remembering the poor acting performance of the mission commander.

"I refuse! That creep disgusted me. I never want to see him again," she complained, just as Paul entered the vast room, also wearing a very peculiar space suit.

HER FRIENDS

It looked like a combat outfit straight out of a dystopian future. This suit, molded to his body, highlighted his athletic and powerful silhouette, ready for action.

Illuminated areas extended along the suit, creating a bluish glow that cut through the black matte surface of the clothing. These glowing patterns animated dynamically, pulsing and lighting up in response to movements and environmental conditions. They added a touch of technological brilliance to the ensemble, while evoking an aura of power.

Specific organic zones integrated into Paul's outfit added an intriguing dimension to his appearance. These parts resembled a kind of breathable synthetic skin, forming circular patches across the garment. They seemed almost alive, with a subtle rhythm of expansion and contraction, as if they were breathing in harmony with him.

As Paul moved, the outfit emitted soft, discreet sounds, like electronic and mechanical crackles. These noises contributed to the mysterious aspect of his attire. Every movement he made was accompanied by these subtle sounds, creating an almost imperceptible symphony with each gesture.

He appeared ready to face an entire army in his combat suit.

"Sara!" he exclaimed upon seeing her awake and alert. He approached her eagerly, asking if he could kiss her.

"Not in a million years, you degenerate! Get away from me, I never want to see you again!" she pushed him away, nearly physically.

Olivia smiled as she approached a drawer filled with eyes of all colors.

Paul pretended to be surprised by her overly emotional reaction.

"Don't play innocent. You know very well what we're dealing with now, don't you?" He moved closer to help her choose her new eye, but she violently pushed him away as much as her strength allowed.

"Don't you dare touch me! And let me out of here. I don't care about your stories and your problems with aliens. Figure it out yourselves!" she shouted, closely examining Paul's space suit.

"Don't say silly things. You're safe with us."

"Stop! Please, stop! Have you seen what kind of state I'm in? Is this what you call being safe?" she shot back as she tried to shift to the edge of the bed but failed. "Damn it, help me! I want to get out of here. I've seen enough! What are those scarecrows?" she asked as four mannequins were brought in on pedestals, their arms and legs slightly spread.

"You need to choose your exoskeleton suit. You can no longer walk by yourself or stand up," Olivia explained with the gentlest tone she could muster.

She paused for a moment, then erupted in rage, screaming and hurling insults as she tried to overturn everything around her.

Paul and Olivia exchanged a swift glance at her hysteria. Paul nodded and stepped out of the room. Olivia activated two articulated arms that seized Sara and pushed her back against the bed. A sedative was administered, and she instantly fell asleep.

Olivia remained by the bedside, contemplative as the equipment was removed from the room. She regretted this situation so much. But they had no other choice.

Merlin

Merlin spacecraft

"Wake up," Olivia whispered softly.

Sara turned to the other side, lying in her bed, a space in her cabin. Olivia tried to wake her two more times, but she didn't seem receptive.

"No, leave me alone, I'm cozy here," she murmured quietly, eager to continue her dream.

"You have to get up, we're going to land soon," insisted Olivia.

"Land?" she finally asked, turning around.

"Yes, we're about to arrive in Paris in a few minutes. After that, we'll go straight to the north pillar of the Eiffel Tower so you can touch it."

"Touch it?" she exclaimed in surprise, her eyes wide open as she noticed she could see much better than before.

"Yes, Paul will explain everything to you. Come on, come with me," suggested Olivia.

"Ah, yes, I remember now. Paul... of course, Paul! I almost forgot about him!" she mumbled as she got up to stand. "Wow! Olivia, am I standing on my own?"

"Yes, look at yourself in the mirror. Do you like it?"

Sara took a few steps to position herself in front of the vertical mirror embedded in the wall of her cabin.

She stood before her reflection, her eyes sparkling with excitement as she scrutinized every detail of her anatomy. The room was bathed in a soft, dim light that accentuated the mysterious beauty of her outfit. The elegant curves of the clothing fit her body perfectly, highlighting her graceful silhouette.

With each movement, organic elements animated the fabric, creating a hypnotic display. Delicate floral patterns seemed to bloom where she placed her hands. The patterns stretched and retracted in harmony with her movements, like flowers blossoming at sunrise.

She couldn't help but smile, her rosy lips reflecting the soft glow of the mirror. Her fingers glided over the fabric, feeling the exquisite texture and softness beneath her hands. The organic elements seemed to respond to her touch, transforming into ever-evolving patterns that danced along the garment.

She leaned slightly forward to admire the most dazzling detail of her attire: tiny luminous fireflies seemed to float around her. They moved gracefully, creating starry patterns on the outfit, as if the stars themselves had come down from the sky to adorn her with their brilliance.

Her eyes sparkled with enthusiasm and wonder as she observed this visual symphony unfolding before her. Her outfit was much more than just clothing; it was a moving work of art, an extension of her personality.

She made a few more graceful movements, crouching with impressive fluidity. Her attire followed each of her gestures with remarkable flexibility. She slowly stood up, her movements always seeming to guide the organic elements that unfolded and retracted seamlessly, like breathing, in harmony with her.

Then, with an almost feline lightness, she quickly turned around, twirling several times as if she were dancing. The whole outfit instantly responded to her changes in direction, creating swirling patterns that seemed to float around her, forming a trail of light. Each of her movements was executed with natural grace. Her confidence grew as she understood: her outfit expressed her completely. It adjusted her balance with extreme precision.

Under Olivia's amused smile, she continued to dance, twirl, and leap, testing the limits of her incredible garment like a child. Her balance was perfect, and she felt in perfect harmony with this creation that faithfully followed her.

She couldn't help but laugh and smile repeatedly as she explored the infinite possibilities of her attire.

HER FRIENDS

"Olivia, seriously, what is this thing?" Sara exclaimed, pointing to her outfit in the mirror as if she had discovered a sacred artifact.

"From now on, it's your best ally," Olivia confided, gently taking her hand to encourage her to follow her to the cockpit.

"By the way, where are we? This place is huge for an airplane!" Sara noted, impressed by the size of the space and the generous dimensions of the corridors they were traversing.

"Well, it's not an airplane. Paul will explain everything to you," Olivia explained.

"Ah, Paul here, Paul there. Thank goodness he's around!" Sara grumbled, talking to herself.

As they walked, Olivia displayed a holographic view of the vessel.

"Wow! We're in here? This is enormous! I've never seen anything like it!" she stammered, taken aback by the unprecedented shapes of the spacecraft.

"Don't worry: no one has ever seen this. Not officially, anyway. It's called Merlin," Olivia continued, closing the visual.

"Who's that?"

"That's its nickname. Merlin," Olivia explained, amused, as she gestured broadly around the area.

Sara stood there, stunned by this vision, approving of the name choice. The place was simply magical in her eyes. They moved through the spacious corridors lined with pipes and circuits of all kinds, adorned with shiny displays and buttons. The dim lighting provided a calm and warm atmosphere. Their footsteps echoed in these endless corridors, where every detail seemed meticulously calculated.

They passed through several rooms, each more fascinating than the last. First, an elegant dining room with immaculate tables awaiting invisible guests. She let out a soft whistle of admiration, asking Olivia what it was doing there. Olivia, in a blasé tone, replied, "It's just the dining room, nothing special."

Their journey continued into a bustling laboratory, with screens displaying complex data and machines with strange shapes. Awestruck, she exclaimed, "Incredible! What is this place?" Olivia replied, still casually, "They put your eye here."

She gently touched the edge of her left eye and blinked several times, as if to feel the synthetic intruder. But everything seemed fine, better than before.

They continued their exploration, reaching an indoor garden where exotic plants flourished in hanging pots. Sara reached out to touch the leaves, marveling at this unexpected marriage of nature and technology. "This is one of my favorite places. It's magical, isn't it?" Olivia asked her. Sara responded with a wide smile, still amazed to find such a space in an airplane. But it wasn't an airplane.

The sound of their footsteps changed as they approached a sparkling pool bordered by Corinthian columns, illuminated by savvy and shifting lights along the edges. Sara exclaimed with contagious joy, "But what do I see? A pool?" Olivia, with a slight smile on her lips, conceded, "Paul loves to splash around in the water!"

"It's absolutely beautiful!" Sara exclaimed.

"Go down and dive, you won't regret it," Olivia replied, stopping for a moment.

"Dive? To see what exactly?"

"Go down. I promise you'll love it!" Olivia assured while pointing to a small ladder leading down to the water.

Sara, though slightly hesitant, ultimately decided to accept this unexpected invitation. After all, swimming in midair was an experience she wouldn't miss telling about.

She cautiously descended the small ladder, slowly moving into the water. However, her surprise was much greater when she realized the water was pulling away from her to create a dry, empty circle around her.

HER FRIENDS

"So, do you like it?" Olivia asked, laughing at the precautions her colleague was taking, discovering for the first time the shield of her spacesuit.

"It's simply magical!" Sara exclaimed, fascinated by this phenomenon. She tried to touch the water with her hands, but it moved away with each motion.

"Come on, let's go. You can enjoy it more later," Olivia invited her, waving for her to join and continue their walk to the cockpit.

"By the way, where are the doctors?"

"Ah, Carlo and Lucas? They are with us on Merlin. You'll probably run into them. Come, follow me."

Moments later, they stood in front of a secure airlock equipped with an iris scanner. Olivia paused for a moment, teased by Sara who was joking about the luxury of this extraordinary place in midair. Olivia replied with a wink before scanning her eyes to unlock the door. It opened silently, revealing Paul busy in the cockpit. He stood up to welcome them. Sara, awe-struck, murmured, "I really didn't expect this." Olivia, unfazed, reassured her with a slight smile: "It's always like this the first time."

"Welcome!" Paul exclaimed, delighted to see her again, especially happy to see her standing after her injuries.

The cockpit of Merlin was a true technological marvel. Upon entering, one was struck by a sense of wonder. The vastness of the room was apparent from the first glance. The walls were made of transparent panels, offering a breathtaking view of the clouds stretching into the horizon.

At the center of the room loomed a gigantic porthole that seemed to comprise a large part of Merlin's hull. This porthole provided a panoramic view, creating a breathtaking experience for those inside.

The lights were omnipresent, reflecting off the immaculate metal surfaces. The cleanliness was undoubtedly maintained with regularity to achieve such a level of tidiness. Illuminated control panels dotted the room, featuring holographic touch screens that seemed to float in the air. Beams of light gently danced around the consoles, creating a captivating atmosphere.

The pilot's seat was a work of ergonomic design, perfectly enveloping the body to ensure optimal comfort. The controls were sleek and intuitive, allowing the pilot to maneuver Merlin with incredible precision and effortless ease.

This place gave the ambiguous feeling of being both tiny and all-powerful. From the suits to the rooms, everything had been designed with a concern for harmony and efficiency. The designer of these things was a true artist.

Returning to reality after those seconds of wonder, Sara felt happy, even physically.

"Thank you, Paul," she said. "Did you see my new flexibility?" she added, performing a pirouette worthy of a ballet dancer. He was impressed by her performance—how could he not be in the presence of such grace?—but he remained cautious.

"Aren't you going to insult me this time?" he asked playfully.

"No, because you're going to drop me off at the airport in Paris, where I'll take a real plane to go straight home. By the way, thanks for this space suit. After everything you've put me through, I think I've earned it," she explained, not waiting for a reaction in return.

Paul pondered while scratching his chin. "Alright, if that's what you want. We land and drop you off at the airport. We'll even pay for your return," he said with a facial expression that revealed no emotion.

"I'm starting to get a sense of you alien hunters. What's the catch?" she challenged Paul.

"Nothing. You're free. I just thought you might agree to help us. I was mistaken," Paul replied, turning back to the control panel.

"I don't like this, Paul. You're trying to make me feel guilty, treating me like a child," she said sadly, under the gaze of Olivia, who seemed well-informed on the subject. Paul didn't respond.

HER FRIENDS

"If you could at least clearly explain what's really going on, maybe I would be more inclined to help. Is that too much to ask?" she continued, with Olivia nodding in encouragement. Paul immediately turned around and stood up from his chair to approach Sara. His movements were so fluid he seemed to be gliding.

"Look at me closely. Do you really believe that it was us who shot at you?"

"Oh no, not necessarily. But it's definitely you who broke my nose," she scoffed.

"Your nose is fixed now, isn't it? What I mean to say is that you were hit by a shot coming directly from the spacecraft we have identified. I understand. For someone not in the know, those words sound like they come from a bad TV series. Yet this is our reality," he explained, casting a glance at Olivia to ask her to leave them alone.

"Please, be more specific. I don't understand why you need me so badly."

"The only thing we know for sure is that we possess a weapon capable of stopping this spacecraft dead in its tracks. And that the ammunition for this weapon is partly made from your DNA."

"So how does your thing work? You take a blood sample, pour a few drops into a bullet, shoot at the spacecraft, and it explodes in space? Did I get that right? We're talking about space werewolves taken down with silver bullets, right?" Sara mocked, punctuating her words with grand theatrical gestures.

Paul was not in the mood to respond to her teasing. He knew the plan had to go off without a hitch if he hoped to fend off this invasion. Like Carlo and Lucas, he would have preferred her help to be voluntary rather than coerced, as Kurtz had asked. For Kurtz, anticipating all risks, even the smallest ones, was essential. He hated surprises.

"It's a quantum suppression cannon: one shot with the right components, and the reality where that spacecraft exists will be annihilated."

"Oh, wow..." she exclaimed, incredulous.

Paul smiled briefly before continuing his demonstration. "We have done calculations to identify which molecular configuration could destroy the structure of this unknown ship. We searched for its weak point, its Achilles' heel. And the result turned out to be a very specific and unique macromolecule: your DNA."

"And boom! No more extraterrestrial spaceship!" she added before bursting into laughter. "Sorry, excuse me, it's just that... it's a bit stressful."

"It's nothing. Take your time. I wouldn't probably do any better in your place," Paul reassured her seriously while watching Sara giggle out of the corner of his eye.

"Okay, okay. It's not very clear, but I more or less understood. But why did they shoot me like a rabbit?" she asked.

"What do you think?" Paul replied, eager to see her reaction.

"I don't know. Let me guess. Your electricity provider made it clear that it was time to pay your bills, or it would be worse next time?" she suggested.

Paul and Sara shared a conspiratorial laugh at this unexpected assumption.

"Joking aside. They shot at you because they're not stupid. On their part, they've understood perfectly well that you are the bearer of their absolute flaw."

"Oh really?" she pretended to be surprised.

"Yes. When I say that you are our only option, I'm not lying. I'm not making anything up."

"They wanted to eliminate me so they could invade Earth unimpeded?"

"It looks that way, yes," Paul confirmed, his face serious.

"Alright. There are two little details that still bother me. How did you know it was my DNA and not the neighbor's? And what exactly are we going to do in Paris at night?"

HER FRIENDS

"The Martians have had access to the DNA of everything living on this planet for a long time," Paul explained.

"Oh really? Did you take samples from everyone?" she wondered.

"No need. We can read DNA from the air for quite some time now. We recently sold this technology to several police departments. They are very enthusiastic."

"Wait, you mean we're all registered because of you?" she asked suspiciously.

"Well, I can see the look on your face. If you want to know everything, we have existed in this specialized institute form for two hundred fifty years and even longer in the form of a brotherhood," Paul explained.

"The Templars!" she exclaimed, raising her arms in discovery.

"Yes, go ahead, mock me. It's easy," Paul replied, slightly annoyed.

"No, keep going. Your thing is fascinating. Actually, no, I don't care. I'm hungry!" she declared, looking around as if searching for a pack of cookies.

"Here, take this," he offered, remotely opening a small drawer containing neatly aligned small bars. "Have one, and you won't be hungry until tomorrow."

"Alright, so what are we doing in Paris?" she asked between chewing her chocolate bar.

"I haven't finished telling you who we are..." Paul said, perplexed.

"Later. Every time I learn something new about you, it gives me a headache. So what are we doing in Paris then?"

"It's very simple: you need to touch the north pillar of the Eiffel Tower," he declared stoically, facing Sara, who lowered her arms.

"And that's it?" she added. She was a bit disappointed that her almost magical space suit and this fantastic trip on the Merlin, the extraordinary ship she hadn't even known about the day before, were only for that.

"Yes, you touch it, and we leave. It's that simple," he confirmed while watching her devour the bar greedily. "Aren't you going to ask me why?"

"I am. And what's the point?" she asked, licking her fingertips.

"Your DNA needs to be completed by this precise vibrational energy. You see, the wrought iron that makes up the metal of the tower originates from the recipes of the best alchemists of King Louis XIV. They had the science of material purity."

"That's fascinating! I can already picture it: I touch the Eiffel Tower and BOOM! My powers are boosted!"

"You're mocking me, aren't you?"

"Yes. How did you guess, sharp one?" she said, bursting into laughter.

"Anyway, your DNA will be enhanced in an astonishing way. There will be other destinations afterward. I'll give you the schedule as we go along."

"You don't trust me?"

"I do, but I don't know them myself. With each transfer of energy, we check if it has properly completed your DNA as planned. And this new configuration tells us the precise place you should touch next, right up to the final configuration we need as ammunition. Are you following me?" he explained.

"Do I have a choice?" she asked.

"No. I mean, do you understand me?" Paul clarified.

"Absolutely not. At least, I'm honest, you see? But I trust you. And you, Paul, do you trust me?" she asked provocatively.

He approached her and held her gaze intensely. "Yes. And I need to protect you, because they will try to kill you by any means necessary. Paris will be our first real battle. We will have losses. And you must stay alive. We have only four days left. In four days, they will be too close. Our weapon will no longer be able to stop them."

HER FRIENDS

"But how do you know I need to touch the north pillar? Why not the south pillar?"

"We only know that you need to touch the wrought iron of the north pillar for a transfer. It's like your level of annoyance. The urgency was to find the exact recipe to move forward. We'll see later why it works. That's already a lot, don't you think?" he explained very convincingly.

"I have a better option: I give you a drop of my blood, you pour it on that damn pillar, and you get my super-boosted DNA back. It's a gift! And in the meantime, I'll go home, because I must say I've seen enough," she replied.

"I'd like that. You'd still be looking for a job and you would never have heard of us in your life. You're scared, aren't you?" Paul asked, amused.

"Honestly? Yes. Try to put yourself in my shoes for a moment."

"You're going to save the world. Do you understand that? You're going to save the world!"

"Do you want me to tell you what I really think, my dear Paul? Do you want? Well, I'm not one of those who believes the world deserves to be saved. If you act like this, with some crazy equipment, discreetly, without any issues, it's because you're protected by the government. The truth is that you're just lowly bureaucrats on a mission to protect a system that makes so much money for your bosses."

"Do you have a problem with that?" he asked, worried.

"Paul, honestly, who doesn't love money?" she said, mimicking a large pile of cash with her arms.

"I see. Don't worry, your share is guaranteed!"

PAUL TOSKIAM

The Tower

Justine and Lydia's Apartment

Lydia rushed out of her room and burst into the living room like a tornado, shouting and startling her mother Justine, who was enjoying the latest episode of her favorite show.

"Mom, Mom! Look at this, the Eiffel Tower is on fire!" she exclaimed, her eyes wide open, pointing at the screen of her phone.

Justine, stunned and disoriented, searched for the remote control and turned on the news. There, they both witnessed a shocking sight: the Eiffel Tower was indeed ablaze, partially destroyed.

Social media was flooded with images posted by people on the scene. Two close friends called them to discuss this incredible event. Even their elderly neighbor joined them, knocking on their door to make sure they had seen what was happening on TV.

They gathered in the living room and began discussing what they were seeing live. The exact causes were still unknown, but the damage was clearly extensive. Justine, taking a deep breath, pulled Lydia into her arms, crying.

"Mom, it's just like in your dream..." Lydia said, as frightened as her mother.

The neighbor looked at them, puzzled about what they were talking about. Lydia briefly explained to him.

"It's impossible..." he murmured, lost in thought. "How can someone dream of such a thing?"

PAUL TOSKIAM

The North Pillar

Eiffel Tower, Paris, France

The esplanade of the Eiffel Tower stretched out before the majestic iron structure like a high-fashion apron. The City of Lights was gradually sinking into an almost mystical silence. The soft glow of the full moon and the street lamps lit up this dreamlike scene. The Seine, calm and serene, reflected the twinkling stars scattered across the night sky.

A few sparse passersby wandered the esplanade, each seeming to have the Eiffel Tower all to themselves. Their footsteps echoed softly on the cobblestones, breaking the night's silence with a discreet rhythm. Some walkers held hands, others roamed alone, lost in their thoughts, while some vendors still vied for the last tourists to finish selling their stock for the day.

A gentle breeze brushed against the trees lining the esplanade, making the leaves softly rustle. The air was imbued with a lingering warmth, and the scent of flowers from the surrounding gardens floated in the air, creating an enchanting atmosphere.

The Eiffel Tower itself stood like a divine iron figure, tall and conquering, proudly anchored on its four pillars. Its silhouette, both massive and graceful, seemed to reach for the stars. Its powerful beacon, rotating at the top and cutting through the clouds, provided a reassuring watch over the city. At this late hour, the tower's light display was but a memory. It no longer sparkled with that characteristic elegance, illuminating the night with golden and silver reflections. Yet, passersby still admired it, even imagining the illuminations despite their interruption. They paused sometimes to take photos, capturing the moment and the memory of this peaceful night in Paris, a night that for some would be the only one of their lives.

The Seine, for its part, was a mirror of calm and serenity. A few barges floated silently on the river, their muted lights barely illuminating the water's surface.

The city around would soon be asleep in this fairy-tale setting. The esplanade of the Eiffel Tower and the Seine formed, as every evening, a magical backdrop, filled with mystery and beauty, where the night unveiled their secret splendor to those who took the time to admire them.

Like a shadow, Sara cautiously slipped through the oppressive darkness that enveloped the Eiffel Tower. The distant glow of the full moon faintly reflected on the rain-soaked metal of the north pillar. She was soon near her goal: to touch this metal, at this spot, with her hand. This action, seemingly so simple, still struck her as ridiculous. How had she gotten herself into this ridiculous story? Yet her heart was pounding in her chest, pumping her blood rapidly through the veins in her neck to her brain. In this astonishing and unusual silence around the monument, she felt her body on high alert.

Every movement, every breath, was imbued with a tension she could not control. Her slender fingers slowly approached the pillar, almost brushing against the cold metal surface. Anxiety gripped her, for she knew—though she didn't truly believe it—that the mere contact of her fingers with the pillar would trigger a series of irreversible events. Once this task was accomplished, she would be extracted from this place she would have loved to explore under different circumstances.

"Try to breathe more slowly," Olivia urged from behind her, positioned above the Champ de Mars and watching.

However, just as her fingers were about to make contact with the metal, a supernatural and terrifying light suddenly manifested before her. A scream of terror lodged in her throat as Sara was propelled into the air with inhuman force. Her dislocated body twirled in the darkness like a leaf in autumn before heavily landing on the Massangis

HER FRIENDS

stone at the base of the pillar and then bouncing back toward the ground.

"Sara. Are you okay?" Olivia asked anxiously.

She was dazed, as if she had hit the pillar with her head. But surprisingly, she was able to get up almost immediately.

"I'm fine. I think my suit saved my life," she replied, glancing around dazedly.

"Behind you!" Olivia whispered urgently.

Sara instinctively turned, and before her stood a silhouette, a creature that defied all rational explanation. There loomed a massive and imposing shadow. It reminded her of a warrior straight out of a nightmare. Its eyes glowed with a demonic light as it fixed its gaze on Sara, as if reading the darkest thoughts of her soul.

The warrior was clad in incandescent weapons, sinister blades strapped to its back. The glowing red aura emanating from these weapons hinted at a supernatural malevolence. In an instant, it began to approach her, its feet barely touching the ground. It levitated with a disturbing grace, showing no apparent effort. Each second it moved closer in the semi-darkness intensified the anxiety gripping Sara.

Breathless, she understood that she had no chance of getting out unscathed. The supernatural man was inexorably drawing near, like the grim reaper coming to claim what was owed to him. She tried to distance herself from this terrifying being, but her legs were still weak, her muscles numbed by the sudden fall.

In a flash, the demonic man was upon her. With a powerful hand, he seized one of the incandescent blades from his back. The sickening light emanating from it reflected in her eyes, and Sara's gaze filled with horror. Thrown back, she watched this brutal figure land before her.

"Get up and jump! Your suit will save you!" Olivia cried out in a panic.

As she lay helpless on the cold ground, the warrior raised the sword with the macabre grace of a gesture executed thousands of times. The metal seemed alive, vibrating with malevolent energy. Just as the blade was about to descend upon her, Sara had one last thought, a silent and naive prayer for the humanity she had tried to save. Then darkness engulfed her.

"Sara!" Olivia cried out in a sob.

The sharp blade descended with deadly precision, cleaving her body symmetrically in half at the waist. Blood gushed from the wound, splattering the cold stone of the Eiffel Tower's pillar and soon washed away by the rain. The silence that followed terrified Olivia, only interrupted by the sound of wind whistling through the tower's metal beams and the patter of raindrops.

The demonic man remained standing, motionless, as if savoring his victory. Then, with a swift motion, he sheathed his bloody sword and drew a dagger. He raised his hand to the sky to arm his arm and separate the head from the torso in one blow. But he stopped abruptly and fell heavily to his knees beside Sara. His chest was pierced by a giant sword with a serrated blade on one side.

His blood gushed from his torso and slid down the blade of the sword that pierced him through and through. Slowly, he raised one knee and turned his head to find out who had dared to provoke him in treachery. As his gaze lifted, he discovered the long black braid, the hooked nails, and the characteristic hateful glare of Admiral Mobo.

He stood there, legs slightly apart with a second sword in hand.

"Admiral Struiz, you should never have done that!" Admiral Mobo said, striding forward to finish him off.

Struiz did not allow himself to be defeated. He leaned forward, drawing out the sword that pierced his body. Then he got back up, seized the bloody sword covered with his own blood, and charged toward Mobo who was coming at him.

The two admirals launched themselves at each other, their swords clashing violently with a thunderous noise. Every strike was infused with bloody rage, sending sparks flying that illuminated the darkness of the night.

"You will pay for the life you took, Struiz! Your arrogance and cruelty will not go unpunished!" Mobo shouted, determined to exact justice for Sara.

Struiz, wounded but undeterred, sneered with contempt. "Jealousy blinds you, Mobo. I will finish the job and help you join her."

The two warriors engaged in a macabre dance of combat, their movements large, fast, and precise, testament to their expertise in the art of killing. The sharp blades whistled through the air, seeking to pierce the flesh of their opponent without restraint.

"You're just an instrument of destruction, Struiz!" Mobo spat with a deep hiss in his throat, narrowly avoiding a blow that could have cost him his life. "Killing mercilessly in the name of power is a despicable perversion!"

Struiz, mad with rage and blinded by his thirst for power, struck back with a precise blow to Mobo's leg. The blade sank deep into the muscle, causing Mobo to scream in pain. But he did not let himself be defeated and retaliated with untamed fury.

"I will prevail! I will prove my worth to the Grand Master!" Struiz roared, forcefully pushing Mobo away with a powerful kick.

In a brilliant flash, the two admirals were locked in a daunting battle, each strike seeming like a declaration of war against the universe itself.

Their blades clashed relentlessly, like two unleashed forces of nature, their bloodied bodies, but their spirits unshakeable. The screams of pain were muffled by the fierce determination that drove them. They soared into the skies, their figures cutting through the air like raging eagles, striking with unrelenting violence. Words had lost all meaning, leaving only the roars of anger that guided them.

Their fates were intertwined in this macabre dance, each seeking to invoke death, but for opposing reasons. In an explosion of rage, their bodies intertwined, releasing a titanic energy that pierced the west pillar from end to end, illuminating the tower with a terrifying light. They replicated this devastating movement, tearing through the north and west pillars in several spots like a destructive hurricane.

Finally, back on the ground, Mobo managed to topple Struiz, pinning him down with an unyielding force. His murderous gaze reflected the incandescent essence of his being as he raised his sword above his head.

"You will die because deep down, you're afraid, Struiz!"

With a steady motion and mechanical speed, Mobo brought down his sword with such power that it split the ground and Struiz's body in two. An explosion of flesh, blood, and entrails stained the horror of the scene and splattered the admiral Mobo. He lifted his head, staring at the Seine, impassive, his face smeared with the blood of his arch-enemy. Silence fell again, broken only by Mobo's rough and triumphant breath as death itself seemed to retreat before the grandeur of this confrontation.

The tumult of battle gradually faded, while Mobo remained there, motionless, staring at the remains of his sworn enemy.

The demons and deep frustrations he had fought, he had just defeated them for good. He felt an inexplicable joy rising within him, a feeling more powerful than life itself: freedom.

But the price he had paid, and one he would still have to pay, was high. The image of Sara, the one he had sworn to protect, tore through his thoughts.

The fight was over, but Admiral Mobo's new inner war was just beginning. He now had to make a difficult decision: continue to fight for justice and freedom, or let madness and violence consume him. The Grand Master would seek to punish him severely through torture, for revenge, and as an example.

HER FRIENDS

He gently knelt near her. Then, he placed his hand on her bloodied remains. He meticulously gathered the two parts of her body. He worked like a butcher handling cuts of meat in the early morning.

Admiral Mobo stood there, Sara's remains in his hands. His mind boiled with rage as he began to drift into daydreams, searching in his unruly imagination for the best scenario for the Grand Master's downfall, once and for all.

With a cold and calculating gaze, Mobo started to devise a bold plan. He knew he had to act with caution, as defying the Grand Master carried great risks. But he was now ready for anything. He knew he could no longer turn back.

He gathered the two pieces and carefully pressed them against each other, aligning them perfectly.

"Come back to me, Sara. Don't leave me alone in this world filled with darkness," he whispered, his eyes filled with tears.

When he finished, he concentrated all his energy in his palms and closed his eyes, murmuring words of power that seemed to echo from ancient times. Suddenly, light began to emanate from his hands, enveloping the lifeless body.

Olivia and Paul, who had rushed to the scene in the hope of saving her, watched this heartbreaking spectacle. Their weapons were aimed at this colossus, ready to take him down.

As the light reached its peak, Sara's body trembled in a wave of spasms and appeared to rebel against death. Her limbs began to move, her eyelids fluttered slightly, and finally, her eyes opened.

"What happened?" she asked, her voice weak but filled with confusion.

"Sara!" Olivia exclaimed, tears of joy streaming down her cheeks.

Admiral Mobo turned to her. He had sensed her presence but had not paid it any mind until then. He stood tall and faced Olivia and Paul, who began to fire at him with two crossed bursts.

She looked up at the bloodied giant, a glimmer of gratitude in her eyes. "Is it you?"

Mobo, struck by the intensity of the gunfire, smiled at her for a moment with intense happiness in his soul. He vanished instantly, as if he had melted into the air itself, in a breath that swept the entire esplanade at the foot of the tower, throwing everyone to the ground.

"Sara!" Olivia cried as she stood up and ran towards her, followed closely by Paul.

"I know him. I've seen him in my dreams," Sara stammered, her voice completely bewildered, as she got up and touched the enormous, still-open scar that ran across her waist.

Olivia helped her walk toward the flaming north pillar to finally touch it at the least ardent spot. Instantly, a ball of energy illuminated Sara's body, contorting as if seized by extreme pain.

Paul, assisted by Carlo and Lucas, collected the remains of Admiral Struiz to take them aboard Merlin.

The majestic Eiffel Tower, like a gigantic iron sentinel ablaze, rose proudly, dressed in a robe of flames in the heart of Paris. In this night that enveloped the City of Light in its dark cloak, the tower became a fiery witness to an extraordinary event, the impact of which would change so much.

At the foot of this iconic landmark, a crowd gathered hastily, drawn by a singular cacophony, a tumult of cries and metallic clatter that abruptly shattered the evening's serenity. The curious and intrigued passersby approached, initially believing it to be an artistic performance or a fleeting spectacle, akin to the celebrations for national day. However, what was about to unfold before their astonished eyes far surpassed all their assumptions.

The Eiffel Tower suddenly had its northern and western feet completely engulfed in flames. And with a deafening metallic crash, it began to tilt terrifyingly toward the Seine, as if it wished to gaze upon its deep waters. An indescribable turmoil soon engulfed the scene, with

HER FRIENDS

emergency vehicles, helicopters, and drones converging in a frenzied whirlwind. Media outlets from around the globe broadcasted live images of this iconic monument, deeply wounded and disfigured. It threatened to plunge entirely into the Seine.

The crowd, now uncontrollable before this astonishing spectacle, was struck by a mix of fascination and dread. Gigantic stampedes caused dozens of deaths and injuries that the emergency services struggled to manage. What unfolded before their eyes had become a massive nightmare. It was a terrifying reality that had turned this evening into an unforgettable night. The extraordinary had overwhelmed the ordinary. The splendor of the Eiffel Tower had been put to the test by distressing forces.

There were talks of an unclaimed attack. The hypotheses regarding the identity of the perpetrators soon multiplied, as numerous as the stars in the sky on this very special night when Admiral Mobo fell forever and madly in love with this human named Sara.

PAUL TOSKIAM

The Passenger

Merlin spacecraft

The cabin was shrouded in semi-darkness, the soft light casting mysterious shadows that danced around Sara and Paul. They stood near the porthole, captivated by the spectacle of the starry night sky. Sara had undergone another surgery, this time performed by the skilled hands of Carlo and Lukas. The two doctors had embarked on a series of tests and examinations in an attempt to unravel the mystery surrounding the miraculous fusion of her two body halves. The complexity of this operation, carried out in record time with bare hands, exceeded their skills, sparking a mixture of fascination and questions.

Physically, Sara felt completely recovered, despite the imposing scar that wound around her waist, just below her navel. However, it was the torment of her memories that troubled her. For the past few hours, everything had been swirling in her mind, creating a whirlwind of emotions and perplexities.

"I don't understand what happened, Paul," she murmured in a trembling voice, the stars faintly illuminating her face. "That guy, I swear, I knew him."

Paul placed a comforting hand on her shoulder, sensing her growing distress. "Calm down. Take a moment to breathe deeply. Otherwise, you might choke."

She fought against a sob, holding back tears that threatened to spill. "I don't know, Paul. It's like I've seen his face before, like I've felt that rage that drove him. I feel like it's linked to my dreams, to the strange visions I've had these past few nights. And I see the pyramids. Paul, I have visions now!"

The silence in the cabin seemed to grow heavier, and each of her words resonated like an unsolvable riddle. Paul's eyes were fixed on her, filled with concern and a multitude of swirling thoughts. "My latest calculations confirm that you absolutely need to make contact with the structure of the Pyramid of Khufu. And as soon as possible to complete the modification of your DNA. You know that's our only hope. I hope everything goes as planned in the end. Otherwise..." he said, letting his sentence hang, marking the weight of uncertainty.

She stared at him, intrigued but empathetic. The conquering and self-assured Paul had given way to a man much less comfortable with this new quality he had to embody: improvisation. The distant stars seemed to watch over them, silent guardians of an uncertain fate.

"Otherwise? We die?" she murmured, the words echoing her own apprehension.

Paul, facing the Milky Way, diverted his gaze from the firmament to plunge into the deep abyss of her eyes. The intensity of his look reflected unfathomable darkness. Doubt grew insidiously within him, like a fleeting shadow slipping into the darkest corners of his soul. He wondered if she was hiding a secret from him, an unspoken mystery lurking in the depths of her gaze.

"I don't know," he whispered, his voice heavy with gravity. "No one knows. But with what happened tonight, the omens are not favorable."

A cold shiver ran down Sara's back. "You look lost, Paul."

"I am," he admitted, revealing his vulnerability. "At The Martian, we have been preparing for this eventuality for a long time. I realize that my fears far exceed my imagination."

Not allowing herself to be overwhelmed by Paul's dismay, she stood tall. A glimmer of boldness shone in her eyes.

"Well, I'm going to show you something that will give you even more chills," she announced, pulling her phone from the jumble of her personal belongings. "Come closer."

HER FRIENDS

The phone, like a lantern in the night, faintly illuminated their faces as she handed him the message sent by Mobo. Her breath caught. "Here, look," she whispered, her voice laced with constant tension.

Paul scanned the message with surprising speed, caught between shock and anger. "Why am I only reading this message now? Were you planning to hide it from me for long?"

She did not back down, holding his gaze, unwavering. "Oh, don't play that game with me, Paul. I'm not your submissive little servant cowering in fear before your anger."

Paul let out a sigh, regretting his previous words. "That's not what I meant."

She took a deep breath, the darkness of the night seemingly merging with her thoughts. "Listen, Paul. Let's set things straight," she stated firmly. "Since I am the cornerstone of your response to these... space entities, I'm also the one who will decide the course of events. From now on, I'm the one who decides."

Paul raised an eyebrow, then suddenly burst into laughter, a laugh that seemed to traverse the starry night like an enigmatic melody. "Decide?" he exclaimed, irony dripping from his voice. "I could settle for keeping a few fragments of your DNA alive and continue our quest without you," he continued, teasing.

She was not intimidated, her gaze anchored in his. "Be careful. I have a protector now. And he is remarkably powerful," she said, referring to the magnificent victory won by Admiral Mobo, to whom she also owed her enigmatic resurrection.

Paul's laughter faded, giving way to deep contemplation. "You're right about one thing."

She fixed him with an intense look. "Oh, which one?"

"He is extraordinarily powerful. Perhaps even too powerful for us."

"Don't be defeatist. I believe we've only witnessed a mere demonstration."

"You seem quite confident."

"No, I don't know. I just imagine that these beings, coming from beyond the stars to destroy each other before our eyes, are doing so purely for pleasure."

"Just for pleasure?"

"Yes. I fear that all beings in the universe come from the same mold: cruel, ready to shed blood to impose their will, by instinct."

"I understand. In any case, it's not me who has muddled your mind like this."

"What are you implying, you..." Paul abruptly interrupted. A series of screams suddenly echoed in the corridors, breaking the silence of the night and plunging them into new uncertainty.

Paul checked the surveillance screens. There was no one outside. Yet more screams resonated, drawing closer.

They cautiously exited the cabin and crept through the corridors. An oppressive silence reigned, only interrupted by strange muffled growls and a putrid stench that permeated the air. Paul tried to get a picture of the other rooms on the Merlin, but he was met with nothing but static. Their curiosity piqued, they decided to head toward the operating room where Carlo and Lukas were performing an autopsy on Admiral Struiz's corpse.

As they drew nearer, the stench intensified, infiltrating their nostrils and sending shivers of horror down their spines. They then discovered, to their shock, at the entrance of the operating room, a pool of thick blood spread across the airlock. Their anxiety grew as they slid the doors open.

And there, before their astonished eyes, unfolded a true nightmare. Carlo and Lukas should have been busy with their task. Yet, they lay dismembered and lifeless on the operating tables soaked in blood and signs of a fierce struggle. The walls bore dark stains, marred by the outpouring of this vital fluid. It was evident that Carlo and Lukas had resisted as much as they could, but they had been ruthlessly torn apart by Admiral Struiz.

HER FRIENDS

Incredulity was written on their faces. They sought to comprehend how this being, presumed dead, could still be alive. Hadn't he been sliced in half by Admiral Mobo at the foot of the Eiffel Tower? Terror consumed them; this obscene violence defied all logic and seeped into their already tormented minds.

She grabbed Paul by the arm, her hands trembling, a sign of sudden, uncontrollable fear. "How is this possible? Do these things never die?" she whispered, her voice filled with despair.

Paul looked at her, tension clearly visible on his face. "I don't know. They are not human. Something much darker and more malevolent lurks behind him."

The oppressive silence that reigned in the room seemed to amplify, leaving them with a bitter taste of powerlessness and despair. They were now facing a threat that they could not even imagine. Their survival was at stake.

"Come on, we need to get out of here," she murmured, her eyes filling with tears. "We have to find Olivia. She must be terrified."

Paul nodded, the same disoriented thoughts swirling in his mind.

"I can't find her on the radar," he said, disappointed and resigned.

Paul and Sara immediately exited the operating room, startled by a fierce growl approaching them. They ran at full speed through the corridors of the Merlin. They were soon pursued by thick screams reverberating through the ship and heavy footsteps rushing in their direction.

They were terrified. They had to find a way to escape.

They turned a corner and found themselves in a storage room. They pushed boxes and cabinets to block the door, but the creature was already there. It kicked down the obstacles and entered the room.

They bolted again, crossing the room into another corridor. They ran as fast as they could, but the creature was still hot on their heels, more stressful than ever.

"We're never going to escape it!" she shouted.

"We'll find a way!" Paul replied. "We just have to keep our cool and stop... stop panicking!"

They ran for a few more minutes, then reached a door. They pushed it open and found themselves in a chamber.

"We're trapped!"

"No, look!" Paul replied.

He pointed to a trapdoor in the floor. They lifted it and descended into a dark tunnel.

The creature followed them. It growled and roared in anger, but it couldn't reach them.

They ran, barely breathing, through the tunnel, hoping it would lead them to safety.

After a few minutes, they came to another door. They opened it and found themselves in the control room. Paul locked the airlock behind them and the double metal protective shutter.

They were relieved to be safe. But they knew the creature was not far behind. They had to find a quick way to escape the ship, as confronting it was not an option.

Paul approached a console and attempted to communicate with the Martian. His hands trembled, and his heart raced. He had never been so scared in his life.

"We're going to try to contact Earth," he said, his voice shaking.

He typed a few keys on the keyboard, then waited.

After a few minutes, a message appeared on the screen.

"I hear you," the message read. "Switch to video. What's happening up there?"

Paul took a deep breath and stared at her, seeking some form of comfort. But she was just as terrified as he was.

"We're in danger," Paul said. "There's a creature on the ship that's pursuing us."

The image of Kurtz Schwartz appeared on the screen. He had a stern expression on his face.

HER FRIENDS

"We're going to land the Merlin near Giza," he said. "I'm sorry, but we can't delay the mission."

They exchanged a furtive glance. They knew it wasn't a good idea. The creature was dangerous, and it could easily escape the ship during the landing.

But suddenly, the airlock of the control room began to tremble under the powerful blows of the creature.

"Kurtz, do you hear that?" Paul asked, frantic.

"Switch to visual, damn it!" Kurtz ordered, wary.

Paul activated the image on the other side of the airlock, and the sight they saw left them speechless.

Admiral Struiz, in tatters, had reformed around the central scar that crossed his entire body, but in a completely makeshift way. The two halves of his body had reattached themselves to form one, but with a significant misalignment. His shoulders were at two different levels, and his face wobbled, with one side higher than the other, totally askew. It was clearly a job that was functional yet completely botched. And it could not be compared to the perfection of the welding done by Admiral Mobo on Sara.

"We've lost Carlo and Lukas. We don't know where Olivia is," Paul explained, anger in his voice. "Kurtz, that thing is going to tear the Merlin apart!"

Kurtz's face displayed a series of emotions in a matter of seconds, ending with a grimace of rage. He looked like he was on the brink of madness.

"There has to be a solution..." he said, lowering his eyes as he never had before.

He exhaled all the air from his lungs to release the unbearable mental burden. He looked at Sara with a sense of resignation and replied tersely: "I'm ready."

She was stunned by Paul, who was psychologically breaking down. She couldn't understand what was happening.

"What's with that look?" she asked. "You sound like a condemned man. What are we doing?" she finally screamed as the blows grew more rhythmic and powerful against the airlock of the control room.

Paul glanced at Kurtz. He could see in his eyes that he was willing to do anything to save the ship.

"Kurtz will fire the beam at the Merlin."

"And?" she asked incredulously.

"That thing is going to die. Ideally, it will be disintegrated."

"Ah, great, the boss microwaving his employees! How original!" she said with a nervous laugh.

"You don't understand. Your DNA is already modified. You will survive," Paul said, tears in his eyes.

She paused for a long moment, silent, her head bowed as the airlock began to give under the blows.

The airlock of the control room finally gave way under the creature's blows. They found themselves face to face with the completely disfigured Admiral Struiz. Minutes seemed to stretch in the agony of waiting.

Suddenly, she realized what Paul had planned. He was ready to sacrifice his own life and Olivia's to save the mission of the Merlin. Paul, Olivia, Carlo, Lukas, all their faces flashed through Sara's mind as she screamed: "NO!"

Paul pushed her behind him to protect her as she resisted, as if she wanted to confront Struiz barehanded.

"Paul... let me go!" she whispered brokenly.

He nodded, his gaze filled with sadness and compassion. She understood that he was willing to do anything to protect what he now considered the most important mission of his life.

The creature moved dangerously toward them, ready to crush them. But before it could reach them, a bolt from the surface struck the Merlin violently. The ship tipped over, losing all stabilization. The

HER FRIENDS

lights flickered, alarms blared, and a powerful beam of light suddenly enveloped Admiral Struiz, stopping him in his tracks.

Paul rushed forward and held her in his arms as she felt the devastating energy of the beam, close to disintegration. This embrace was their last moment together, filled with tenderness and despair.

"I love you," Paul whispered in her ear.

Paul's words etched themselves in Sara's heart, like a metal stake leaving an indelible mark on stone.

The beam reached its peak, and an explosive burst of blinding light shattered the darkness of the control room. The force of this devastating energy threw them apart, causing them to crash violently onto the floor.

When she reopened her eyes, silence reigned. The creature was gone, and she could not perceive Paul. She rushed out of the control room, her heart racing, searching for him, praying he was still alive.

Her eyes filled with tears when she saw his peaceful but lifeless face. The beam had taken him, sacrificing him to save the others.

There were no bodies, no growls, no crashing sounds.

"Sara. The mission continues."

Those were the futile words of Kurtz that reached her from the control room terminal.

She knelt down. She murmured disjointed words in a trembling, sorrowful voice. They had just given their lives without a second thought. She knew he had given his life to save theirs, and she would never forget it.

She got up and instinctively ran through the corridors in hopes of finding Carlo and Lukas in the operating room. Each time she passed by one of the control screens, Kurtz's image appeared, urging her to pull herself together and return to the control room. He said he would guide her. She ignored everything. It was a desperate race, as deep down she knew she would find no one else on that ship.

PAUL TOSKIAM

The Fate of Mobo

Flagship

Back in his quarters, Admiral Mobo was summoned for an immediate audience with the Grand Master. Without taking the time to relax or change, he followed the direction indicated by the close guard.

The heavy footsteps of Admiral Mobo echoed through the dark corridor leading to the Grand Master's council chamber. The cold white marble seemed to close in around him, accentuating every inch of the path he walked. His heart beat with a feverish intensity, on the verge of exhaustion, as tumultuous thoughts clashed in his tormented mind. Like raging waters ready to engulf his sanity, they threatened to overwhelm him. He had come here fully aware that this audience would play a decisive role in the course of his life, but was he truly ready to face the consequences of his own actions? Or was it the moment for him to put an end to his suffering, to finally free himself from his tormentor?

Admiral Mobo, despite his many recognized and envied qualities, did not know how to make the right decisions. That was the burden he had carried since his childhood in the vast plains of Orion. A place he could not forget. Where his mother and father had tragically lost their lives before his childish eyes. They were victims of a brutal murder perpetrated by the bloodthirsty Voldaves. His survival was due only to the Grand Master, who had taken in orphans like him, making them his most valiant servants.

But like so many others in the universe, Mobo had failed to overcome the chains of his past. He had simply buried his traumas deep within himself, unable to confront them head-on. His soul was mired in that tumultuous hell of hatred and love for the Grand Master, a duality that consumed him day after day, relentlessly. It was an emotional burden he had carried for far too long, one that had become increasingly unbearable each day, and yet it had shaped every part of his being. As he walked down that endless corridor, Mobo remembered his darkest moments. Times when he would hit his head against the walls until it bled, in the hope of expelling the pain that consumed his existence.

He closed his eyes and regained his confidence, clenching his fist and raising his chin forward. He had lived as a warrior, and he would not accept fear, not today, nor ever. Moving forward with determination, he prepared to face the fate that awaited him on the other side of those imposing doors. His gaze was filled with unwavering resolve. He knew deep down that he would soon have to break the chains that held him prisoner to his own past—if the Grand Master allowed him to live. The hour of truth had come, and Admiral Mobo had decided to live up to this moment, for honor.

Since defeating Admiral Struiz, the protégé, Mobo had not felt the slightest remorse. The fleet was his home, his only universe, and he had merely sacrificed one of their own to better serve his purpose: that burning desire to save Sara, the innocent human caught in a galactic hurricane that overwhelmed her.

Burdened by all these thoughts, Admiral Mobo had found the infallible recipe to stir his mind to a boil as he crossed the gigantic doors of the council chamber. The room, although familiar, always appeared vast and austere, adorned with banners decorated with ancient symbols. Sitting on his throne, the Grand Master awaited him, his gaze cold and piercing. His deep voice resonated in the chamber, sending shivers down Mobo's spine. The voice of his surrogate father.

"Admiral Mobo, you are finally here. Step closer."

Mobo advanced with hesitant steps, feeling the sweat bead on his forehead.

"Come closer that I may behold your body in the light."

Mobo stepped a few more paces to stand directly under the beam of light illuminating the front of the throne.

HER FRIENDS

"The depth of your wounds speaks of a hard-fought battle, Admiral Mobo," commented the Grand Master as he leaned over Mobo's many scars. They crisscrossed the admiral's exceptional musculature. In places, his armor remained intact. In others, his bare, thick skin glistened with sweat under the harsh light.

"Grand Master, I am here to face the consequences of my actions," Mobo declared in a calm and resigned voice, though his inner thoughts struggled amidst the chaos.

The Grand Master fixed Mobo with a scrutinizing gaze, examining every inch of his face. But Mobo averted his eyes, feigning an expression of humility and regret. He forced himself to hold his head high, trying not to let the guilt that gnawed at him show.

"Admiral Mobo, the fleet is united, and we do not tolerate acts of treachery," the Grand Master said in a grave tone. "You have eliminated one of our own without permission, and that cannot go unpunished."

Mobo nodded, masking his thoughts as best as he could. "I understand, Grand Master. I am ready to accept any punishment you deem just."

Silence fell in the chamber. Mobo felt the piercing gazes of the other council members, all ready to condemn him for his actions. But he refused to give in to panic. He could not afford to lose his footing now.

"Mobo, you have proven your worth by defeating Admiral Struiz. He was too weak an opponent for you," the Grand Master said, catching Mobo off guard. "I am proud of you," he announced in a deep, slow voice.

The admiral could not maintain the intense gaze of the Grand Master. He felt those words wrapping around his heart, tugging him in every direction.

"There is no escaping your duty, Mobo. Love, friendship, all that matters little when it comes to conquering galaxies. You have pledged allegiance, and you owe me obedience," the Grand Master declared in a voice that grew darker.

"Master, I beg of you..." Mobo submitted, kneeling before the Grand Master's demanding gesture. The council approved of this act.

"Mobo, you will personally bring me this human, dead or alive. I need her without delay. She must not touch the Great Pyramid. They are using her augmented DNA to calibrate a weapon that could disrupt us."

"I understand, Grand Master."

"Then we will destroy this insignificant planet. We must be certain that no other source of her DNA can come to light. Put my mind at ease—do they not yet know how to leave their rock, do they?"

"No, Grand Master. They are just starting down that path."

"Your interest in this primate world is troubling, Admiral."

"Sara does not deserve this. She does not deserve any form of harm. Can't we find another solution?" Mobo pleaded, looking up at the Grand Master.

A mocking smile spread across the Grand Master's lips, revealing his hundreds of sharp, stalagmite-like teeth. He rose from his throne in a tremor that shook the entire room and approached Mobo. Each of his steps startled the council members, who, fascinated, murmured among themselves. With a cold hand, he grasped Mobo's chin, forcing him to look him straight in the eye.

"Mobo, by obeying my orders, you will finally be able to lead this galaxy you cherish so much. But refuse, and you will lose everything. Sara will be condemned and you will forever be a simple outcast, without power or influence. Reflect, Mobo, and make your choice," he threatened in a cavernous voice.

The Grand Master's words echoed in Mobo's mind like thunder rumbling in the depths of the ocean. He felt the pressure intensify and his own power slipping away. He was trapped.

HER FRIENDS

Mobo felt the beats of his heart in that suddenly very quiet chamber. The seconds seemed to stretch into eternity. He faced that intimate enemy he feared above all: the choice.

After a long moment of contemplation, he lowered his eyes. His shoulders sagged, and resignation was written across his face.

"I accept, Master. I will obey your orders," he murmured in a broken voice.

A satisfied smile stretched again across the Grand Master's lips. He released his grip on Mobo's chin and stepped back, pleased with his victory.

"Very well, Mobo. You will prove yourself worthy of leading the Milky Way, as they call it," he declared with a hint of disdain for Earth in his voice.

Mobo remained kneeling for a few more moments, his heart heavy with sorrow and his thoughts still muddled. He had agreed to do evil to gain power, but at what cost?

What was the Grand Master's real ambition?

The Pyramid

Giza, Egypt

Justine and her daughter Lydia were on vacation in Egypt. They had booked a room in a charming little hotel. The terrace offered them a breathtaking view of the three pyramids of Giza, silhouetted on the horizon. Justine felt, in an indescribable way, that she was meant to be in this place at this moment. Her nightmares—some of which were prophetic—had not shown her any pyramids. No, this time it was more vague, less demonstrative, perhaps even more unsettling. She hadn't even mentioned it to her daughter. What they both saw and experienced that night changed their fate.

The starry sky dressed the night in magic, and the full moon cast its peaceful glow over this millennia-old landscape. Justine, immersed in her fragrant bath, savored this moment of relaxation before heading to bed. Lydia was reviewing the performance of her social media posts to decide which images she would take the following day. For a few seconds, she had noticed a light in the corner of her field of vision, but had paid it no more attention than that, too focused on her numbers. However, the increasing intensity of the glow forced her to leave her screen in great frustration and turn her head toward the pyramids.

She fixed her gaze on the horizon several times. She immediately pointed her phone at this impossible scene and zoomed in as much as she could on what was unfolding before her, carefully pressing record.

"Mom... Mom... MOM!" she soon yelled, overcome with intense panic.

Justine raised an eyebrow, thinking her daughter was playing one of her usual pranks.

"Mom! Come see the pyramids! Something is happening!" Lydia stammered, stepping back, her hands trembling as she clutched her phone.

HER FRIENDS

"What is it? I'm quite comfortable here," Justine replied, lounging in the fragrant water and thick foam.

"I swear, come see! They're floating!" Lydia tried to explain, her breath quick and shallow.

"Stop talking nonsense, Lydia. If you want to ask me something, just say it. No need to panic," Justine responded, reluctant to leave her delightful bath.

But Lydia insisted. As she abruptly entered the bathroom, her face wore an unmistakable expression. "Mom, I swear! It's terrifying! Come see!"

Intrigued, Justine asked, "What's going on? You seem worried?"

Without saying another word, Lydia grabbed her mother's wet hand and yanked her out of the water so she would follow immediately. "Stop complaining! You're hurting me!" Justine grumbled as she was pulled out of the water against her will and quickly wrapped herself in a towel. Lydia continued to tug her mother by the hand, her bare wet feet leaving damp tracks on the wooden floor.

Once on the terrace, Justine was captivated by the sight of the Great Pyramid of Khufu, which still stood in its usual place, but several dozen meters above the ground. "Mom, what is that?" Lydia asked, huddling close to her mother in search of immediate comfort.

Justine remained still, staring at the spectacle her mind struggled to comprehend. The Great Pyramid. Unlike similar structures, it stood out for its size, splendor, and enigmatic beauty. Illuminated as if by magic, the pyramid was bathed in vibrant lights that blended with the incandescent, multicolored patterns, creating a supernatural aura around it.

The beams of light, resembling magical bolts, danced across its walls, giving it an almost transparent appearance. This hypnotizing effect revealed the secrets deeply embedded in its ancient bowels. Mysterious tunnels and corridors extended, interweaving and losing themselves in the darkness. Elegantly sculpted ramps appeared to guide those who dared venture into this enchanting underground world.

But what surprised Justine even more was the strange movement of the pyramid itself. Slowly, as if driven by an invisible force, it rotated on itself, revealing different facets of its structure. It was then that one could marvel at the complexity of its design, each detail meticulously considered by its builders.

And at times, like a celestial acrobat, the pyramid seemed to roll over itself. It was as if it were playing with the laws of physics, challenging all established certainties. Justine began to cry, never taking her eyes off it.

"Mom, what's wrong with you?" asked Lydia, concerned to see her mother in this state.

"It's wonderful!" Justine murmured, holding her daughter tightly.

The boundary between reality and illusion had dissolved. The stars, distant in the sky, seemed to applaud this celestial pirouette, while the dunes around the pyramid almost mirrored its movement, in rhythm with it, complicit in this magical ballet.

The Great Pyramid offered a journey into another world, an experience that transcended reality and carried the mind to uncharted territories.

Animated discussions emanated from the street below, followed by honking horns, and gradually, an uproar became increasingly present. Something extraordinary was happening before the incredulous eyes of Justine, Lydia, and all the people present that evening around this mysteriously floating pyramid.

"A helicopter! Two!" Lydia shouted, pointing excitedly at the flying machines, their searchlights trained on the pyramid.

"Come on!" Justine ordered, pulling Lydia by the hand to get her to safety. Then she rushed back to find her phone to capture this unique scene. Lydia, remaining in the living room, watched her mother with a mix of fear and wonder. "Mom, that's enough! I already have

HER FRIENDS

everything I need!" she protested, seeing her mother acting like a filmmaker.

Justine turned to her daughter. "You didn't film the helicopters!" she said, returning to the living room and then to her bedroom, where she dressed in seconds.

"Lydia, come here! We're going."

Lydia observed her suddenly agitated mother, pacing back and forth, hastily throwing some things into her large bag. Justine, usually pragmatic, felt an irresistible force within her. It was something new and inexplicable that propelled her toward the unknown. She grabbed the keys to their rental car and dragged Lydia with her to the reception area. There was no one downstairs. Everyone was on the street in a frantic tumult of people running in all directions, blocked cars, and wailing sirens in the nearby neighborhood.

"It's blocked. We won't be able to get through!" Lydia noted at a glance.

"We'll take a detour on foot. We'll find a way! We don't separate!" Justine ordered, determined to cross the area to get as close as possible to the pyramid.

PAUL TOSKIAM

The Jump

Merlin spacecraft

"Kurtz, I don't know how to parachute!" she screamed, panicked at the thought of the void.

"It's time to learn, my pretty," Kurtz replied, amused, as he played a video showing the basics of parachuting.

"I'm not YOUR PRETTY! Who do you think you are?"

Kurtz paused for a moment, then continued: "The parachute is in the compartment I just opened for you. Pay close attention to the video. You have the dorsal and ventral parachutes. Watch the movements carefully. Your life depends on it."

She watched the video, which seemed to be from fifty years ago. Part of the Merlin's control system had burned out during the assault to eliminate Admiral Struiz, and it could no longer land. She knew she had to put aside etiquette this time and focus on these vital movements.

"We're four minutes from the jump point. The Merlin will then be disintegrated by our ground control," Kurtz explained, increasing Sara's pressure and anxiety.

She found herself in an unknown and uncomfortable situation, similar to astronauts needing to act precisely in a completely hostile environment. She hated this situation and hated this job. Yet, she had no choice. She watched that awful video with the utmost attention.

"Please look at me," Kurtz asked. She positioned herself in front of the camera, putting on her parachute while intermittently staring at it.

"Your space suit will ensure a safe landing. Once on the ground, your primary objective is to reach the Great Pyramid. Nothing should divert you from this goal. Your secondary objective is to stay alive," Kurtz stated in a calm and soothing voice.

"That sounds easy when you put it like that," she joked, though fear made her shiver to her core.

"Our friends are not here to be kind. The last time they came, most living species disappeared from the surface of the Earth. Their ships may look simple, but they are actually formidable war fortresses disguised as mere rocks in space."

"Stop! I'm already panicking enough. Is my parachute properly on?" she asked, spreading her arms and legs while spinning around.

"You don't have time to reach the drop hatch. I'm going to hold the Merlin in a hover and detach the entire right side of the window, right in front of you. You'll need to jump immediately. I will give you more instructions during your descent."

"Kurtz, do you have children?" she asked, leaving Kurtz stunned.

"One daughter and two grandsons," he replied, still taken aback.

"Then I'll do this for them, Kurtz. So they can carry on what you've started," she declared in a voice so solemn that she surprised herself.

Kurtz's eyes no longer blinked. His short breaths were audible. "You can count on me. Get away!"

The window detached at the designated spot, and with a piercing scream, her jaw clenched, she slid through the opening and dove into the void. Her body immediately began to spin as she continued to scream.

HER FRIENDS

Dad's call

Great Pyramid, Giza

"Dad, what are you doing there?" Sara asked, her voice laced with surprise and concern as she sought to locate the familiar tone of her father, George.

"I finally managed to reach you. Your number went to voicemail. Listen carefully, sweetheart, I have a man who..."

"Dad! Stop, not now. I'm parachuting down to the majestic pyramids of Giza!" she exclaimed, her excitement making her voice slightly breathless.

"What? What are you doing parachuting?" George replied, his voice trembling with worry.

"It's too long to explain, Dad. I'm on a crucial mission. I'll be landing in a few seconds," she answered, her tone resolute despite the urgency of the situation.

"Sara, listen to me, a giant of a man came to our house. He ransacked the whole kitchen and left me a diamond the size of an egg. He was looking for you, my angel!" George uttered these words with palpable urgency and distress, his breath short.

Her father's words echoed like thunder in Sara's mind. She instinctively understood that events were spiraling dangerously, threatening the safety of her loved ones. The frantic beating of her heart intensified as her mind raced with tumultuous thoughts.

A shiver ran down her spine just as her feet were preparing to touch Egyptian soil; a multitude of emotions overwhelmed her, an explosive mix of excitement and fear. As she felt the contact with the ground, Sara realized she was at a crossroads, facing a challenge that would mark a turning point in her life.

"Dad, I'll call you back, I need to land without crashing!"

"I love you, my angel!" George shouted, helpless.

HER FRIENDS

She had always been an adventurer at heart, but she never thought she would experience a moment as incredible as this one. Her body stabilized as she descended above the majestic expanse of the Giza plateau. She became aware of the exceptional beauty surrounding her.

Suspended in the air, she gazed at the pyramids standing before her like immortal guardians of time. Their imposing silhouettes seemed to point to a specific spot in the starry sky, shining brilliantly on that clear night. She felt small and insignificant in the face of this grandeur, yet also transported by the mystical energy emanating from the millennia of history in this place.

As she continued her parachute descent, she felt a wave of shivers run up her spine, creating a sensation of lightness. She closed her eyes and let herself be carried by the air currents, feeling almost like a floating feather in the wind.

Suddenly, her imagination took over. She was no longer just descending in free fall. She now envisioned herself flying, like an agile and graceful bird weaving through the air. She executed fluid and harmonious aerial movements, gliding effortlessly between the pyramids.

She opened her eyes and realized with amazement that her dream had become reality. She was indeed flying, her parachute having transformed into majestic wings. She approached the pyramids, almost brushing them with her fingertips.

She then decided to follow her instincts and overflowing imagination. She steered toward the largest of the pyramids, that of Khufu, and dove into its mysterious depths. As she explored the dark corridors, she could feel the ancient history resonating through the stone walls. She could almost hear the whispers of the pharaohs and priests who had once resided there.

Ascending to the surface, she glided along the smooth sides of the pyramid of Khafre, which seemed to almost shine among the stars. She let herself be carried by the wind, sliding along the walls as if they were her own. She felt powerful and free, in perfect harmony with the elements surrounding her.

The pyramid of Menkaure stood before her, almost beckoning her to explore it. She was drawn in by its mysterious allure and dove into its enclosure. She was dazzled by the treasures it held, richly decorated sarcophagi, and vibrant frescoes. She felt privileged to discover them up close, in solemn silence.

Then she moved away from the pyramids and approached the Sphinx, which gazed out at the horizon with its enigmatic stare. She gently landed beside the majestic creature, feeling its aura of power and wisdom. She could almost hear its words, like secret whispers revealing the mysteries of this ancient place.

Time seemed to stand still as she floated in the wind, savoring every moment spent in this sacred realm. She knew that this experience would remain engraved in her mind forever, and that she had been blessed to explore the pyramids of Giza from every possible angle, as if she were a flying dolphin.

"A flying dolphin?" she shouted aloud as she realized the ground was approaching rapidly.

HER FRIENDS

The Reunion

Great Pyramid, Giza

Sara was completely unsettled by this impromptu conversation with her father. Her mind was racing, replaying childhood memories with him. She felt helpless as she listened to her father sounding panicked on the other end of the phone. The fear in his voice was palpable, and she would have given anything to be by his side, to comfort him.

As she was dangerously nearing the ground, her heart was pounding fiercely. This first parachute descent was proving to be an intense and exhilarating experience. Thankfully, her spacesuit managed the landing on its own, coming to a smooth stop upon contact with the ground.

Upon landing on the plateau, she felt a strange sense of grandeur. She was only a few dozen meters away from the majestic and iconic Great Pyramid. A satisfied smile spread across her face as she admired the beauty of this wonder she had never seen with her own eyes.

However, her moment of tranquility and reverie was quickly interrupted by the shouts of the guards who were already chasing her. She knew she couldn't afford to waste any time; she needed to act and fast. With no instructions from Kurtz, who seemed to be unresponsive, she quickly decided to get rid of her parachute by tossing it behind her, hoping to slow down her pursuers.

Gaining momentum, she sprinted as fast as she could, her heart racing even faster. The guards were swift and determined to protect this architectural gem from overly eager tourists. They were likely fed up with clickbait mercenaries and thrill-seeking couples. The adrenaline continued to push her forward. To her surprise, her desire to succeed in this mission grew stronger. She understood that she was participating in a battle against a merciless invader. She had also witnessed her fellow soldiers falling for the cause. There is always a moment of truth in

HER FRIENDS

a human life—a moment when certainty is upended, and the opportunity to achieve something greater than oneself arises. She had just reached that moment, her moment. And she embraced it fully, accepting all its demands and all its consequences.

She knew that if she could reach the Great Pyramid, she would be safe, at least for the time being. She just had to touch it, even briefly, and then leave as quickly as she could. Her legs burning, she was getting closer to her goal, breathless but determined not to give up.

The guards were now only a few meters behind her, the sound of their footsteps resonating in the silence. She could feel their presence, almost their warm breath on her neck. However, she refused to be caught.

As her last remaining strength seemed to abandon her, she made a final effort and, with a powerful leap, she covered the last few meters that separated her from the edge of the Great Pyramid. Desperately clinging to the rough stones, she hoisted herself up to reach a small platform, out of the grasp of the exhausted guards. They were tough and refused to concede defeat. They too were on a special mission.

Victory was hers, at least for the moment. Sara would catch her breath, quickly assessing her options. She needed to find a way to progress to the first corner block of the pyramid without attracting the guards' attention. She felt both exhausted and exhilarated by the incredible adventure that awaited her.

"Ready?" murmured Kurtz impatiently.

"Oh, there you are! Where have you been?" she replied, a thrill of excitement racing down her spine. "I'm ready. One last sprint and I'm there!"

Kurtz took a deep breath, scanning the terrain in front of her. "Okay. The first guard is to your right, behind that tall column. Wait for him to turn his back, then move quickly to the next cover."

She moved stealthily, her heart pounding in her chest. She took advantage of the moment when the guard turned the corner to hide behind an ancient pillar covered in hieroglyphs. She could feel the massive, imposing presence of the pyramid drawing nearer as she advanced.

"Now! There's a group of guards in front of you, at ten o'clock. Create a distraction by throwing a small stone in the opposite direction. When they turn away, seize the opportunity to slip between them."

A sly smile spread across Sara's face as she spotted a stone a few steps away. She picked it up gently and skillfully tossed it in the opposite direction. The guards all turned towards the noise, giving her a safe, if temporary, passage.

She moved quickly, hiding behind each dark corner. Her heart raced as she drew closer to the Great Pyramid, like a fearless explorer.

Kurtz continued to give her precise directions, avoiding the patrolling guards in groups, passing behind the colossal stone statues. Finally, she stood just a few steps away from the majestic and mysterious Great Pyramid towering before her. She tilted her head back to admire the top of the monument, nearly losing her balance.

"You're almost there," murmured Kurtz with a note of admiration in his voice. "Now, move slowly, without sudden movements or unnecessary noise. Let your instincts guide you until your hand reaches the surface of the pyramid."

She advanced cautiously, as if walking on burning coals. She could feel the breath of the pyramid against her skin, beckoning her to come closer. It was an irresistible force. She extended her trembling hand toward the surface of the pyramid. An electric thrill coursed through her body as her fingers brushed against the surface of the corner stone.

Sara's DNA activated immediately, radiating a brilliant light all around her. Just like with the Eiffel Tower, she could feel the power of the pyramid flowing into her, altering her being in indescribable ways.

Kurtz, awestruck by the sight, couldn't help but smile. "You did it! You touched the Great Pyramid and became the force we needed!"

HER FRIENDS

She stood motionless, bathed in golden light, her mind ablaze with newfound knowledge. She was ready to face the world and accomplish extraordinary things.

"Hide! Quickly!" shouted Kurtz, nearly suffocated by the urgency of the situation.

Dizzy, Sara frantically looked around but couldn't focus on anything. She was still reeling from the unprecedented surge of energy that had taken over her body.

The guards, intrigued by the strange light, rushed towards her. Kurtz whispered through gritted teeth: "He's on the other side of the pyramid. Run!"

As she rounded the corner of the pyramid, she came face to face with the imposing silhouette of Admiral Mobo, appearing as if conjured from thin air. He stood there at the other corner of the pyramid, silent, like an apparition.

She froze, taken aback by this unexpected reunion with Mobo. She took in his imposing stature and his hair flowing freely, brushing the ground.

The guards grabbed her and demanded she speak, wanting her to explain her presence. "What's your name? Which hotel are you staying at?" one of them asked in an inquisitive tone. Another, caught up in the action, struck her in the stomach to subdue her as she struggled to break free.

Admiral Mobo approached them with astonishing speed, seemingly gliding or flying just above the ground.

He must have thought he was impressing the guards with this display of power, but they only grew more aggressive and began firing at him. Their crossfire momentarily knocked Mobo off balance, but he regained his composure and calmly advanced towards them, as if nothing had happened. One of the guards shouted a brief command, and they threw grenades that exploded around him. They had abandoned Sara, allowing her to escape as she ran for all she was worth, straight ahead.

She ran as fast as she could, away from the place where the guards and Admiral Mobo were engaged in fierce combat. Her mind was filled with confusion and anxiety about the situation she was in. She knew she had to find a way to hide and protect herself, but she couldn't shake the question of why Mobo was so determined to find her.

After a few minutes of frantic running, she found refuge behind a pile of rocks. She tried to catch her breath, but her heart was pounding so hard that it felt like it would explode out of her chest. She knew she couldn't stay still here, so she began to think about her next move.

However, just moments later, a massive figure appeared in front of her, tightening her chest. It was Mobo, and he was there, relentless. She crouched down and silently pleaded to remain unseen, hoping he would simply walk past her. But deep down, she knew that wouldn't happen.

Mobo approached slowly and stood in front of her, his intense gaze fixed upon her. She could see in his jet-black eyes an unfathomable power and a hint of sadness. Taking a deep breath, she gathered her courage and faced him.

"Why are you hunting me? What have I done to you?" she asked, her voice trembling yet resolute.

Mobo remained silent for a moment before responding in a grave tone, hissing some words: "The Grand Master ordered that I bring you back, dead or alive. He believes you are a threat."

Sara felt a chill of foreboding wash over her. In that moment, she understood that her Martian allies were not joking. She should have listened to them, believed them. Perhaps they would still be alive. Her thoughts were muddled. She couldn't concentrate, lost between a flood of questions and the visceral fear that knotted her stomach.

HER FRIENDS

"I am not a threat," she said, her voice now filled with frustration. "I'm just a seeker of truth. All I want is to understand what's happening here."

Mobo seemed hesitant but remained impassive. "You are a weapon. I must take you back with me," he said, hissing through clenched teeth as he extended his hand toward her.

Tears welled in her eyes as sirens blared in the distance and groups of vehicles approached their position.

She didn't deserve this. She didn't deserve to be hunted and captured. But she knew she had to fight, for her life and for the truth.

"Inform your Grand Master that I will not surrender without a fight," she declared firmly.

Mobo seemed surprised by her resistance but nodded slowly. "Then I will have to kill you."

With those words, Mobo turned and walked away, this time with heavy steps, as reinforcements reached them and opened fire on him.

"Sara, do you copy?"

"Kurtz? Damn! You're never here when I need you. It's a mess here. He wants to take me with him!" she gasped.

"Calm down. I'm going to help you."

"About time!"

"I didn't catch your conversation. What did he say?"

"He says I'm a weapon."

"Holy shit... We need to move faster. A vehicle is waiting for you down below. It will take you to our local institute. I'll be there in thirty minutes. I'll meet you there."

She listened closely to Kurtz's instructions while watching the guards' movements. She knew she had to act quickly and efficiently to avoid being captured. As bullets whizzed around her, she searched for an opening to slip through discreetly.

She spotted a gap in the defense line and stealthily made her way through the bushes to reach the all-terrain vehicle. She could hear the sound of helicopters closing in on Mobo, and she hoped that it would draw the guards' attention, allowing her to move undetected.

When she reached the vehicle, she felt relieved to see that the driver was already waiting, ready to go.

She needed to get out of the city and head to the local institute. A wave of relief washed over her. She knew she had narrowly escaped something terrible.

The sky was darkened by the constant barrage of gunfire, while Mobo, the powerful war chief, struggled to maintain his footing. His body was battered, and his mind was tormented by the rage burning within him. Each explosion shook the ground, sending debris and dust swirling into the air.

But Mobo had a clear purpose in mind. His fury pushed him to summon all his remaining energy against the majestic pyramid standing proudly before him. His muscles tightened, charged with a supernatural power that seemed to grant him the strength of a titan.

He extended his trembling hand, filled with tension and anger, and a brilliant light erupted from it. The arc of energy surrounded the pyramid, creating an invisible barrier of protection. The millions of limestone blocks, once immobile and anchored to the ground, began to rise slowly, maintaining their stacked structure as if they were floating in the air. Soon, a chilling silence settled over this makeshift battlefield. The soldiers, frozen in fear, watched the scene in disbelief.

The gunfire abruptly ceased, almost as if chaos itself had held its breath. Fighters exchanged perplexed glances, unable to comprehend what was unfolding before them. Whispers spread among the soldiers, marking their growing fear in the face of this display of power.

Ignoring the inquisitive looks, he focused all his attention on his task. His muscles tensed as he lifted the pyramid into the air, defying the laws of gravity. His eyes shone with a dark, terrifying glow, fixed on the monument he was manipulating from a distance like a toy.

HER FRIENDS

Every movement was laborious, every breath a painful gasp. But he persisted with tenacious resolve, his almost magical strength allowing him to tame the dark forces that had seemed to dwell within him forever. The pyramid slowly glided through the sky, its imposing mass defying all logic.

The soldiers, once so confident and brave only moments before, now sensed the presence of an unknown and terrifying power. Their weapons felt heavy and useless in their trembling hands. Their morale crumbled, giving way to intense fear as Mobo continued to elevate his precious cargo to celestial heights.

Suddenly, a gentle breeze began to blow, carrying with it a murmur of awe and terror. The fighters watched in amazement as the incredible spectacle unfolded before them, realizing that Mobo was more than just a mere warrior. He was a being of extraordinary power, linked to mysterious forces beyond human understanding.

The pyramid finally reached its apex, majestically floating in the air. Mobo himself appeared transfigured, radiating an aura of dark, powerful energy. He could no longer bear the weight of his superhuman feat, and he collapsed abruptly to the ground, exhausted and broken.

This makeshift battlefield had become as calm as the desert at midnight. Only the sound of helicopter rotors spinning in the distance broke the moment. The soldiers stared at the pyramid suspended in the air, unsure of how to react to this unparalleled display of strength. No military manual had ever imagined such a tactic. Their minds were nearly paralyzed. Panic froze them. They even questioned their own fight.

In a final gasp of pain, Mobo managed to lift himself slightly, gazing at the fruit of his labor. He had accomplished his objective, even at the cost of his own battered body. His breathing was labored, punctuated by deep wheezes, as if he might cough up his lungs, and sweat and mingled blood flowed down his face.

With a blinding flash of light, the pyramid descended slowly to the ground. The soldiers were dazzled by this majestic apparition, but also relieved to see the suspended threat dissipate. They had witnessed an act of bravery and power unprecedented, one that would challenge their worldview.

Mobo, exhausted but proud, stood there, watching as the pyramid resumed its original position. His body gradually recovered strength while his mind buzzed at the magnitude of what he had accomplished.

The battlefield awoke from its catatonic state, the fighters picking up their weapons, but with an entirely new perspective. They had been witnesses to a miracle, a demonstration of power that surpassed them all. And the legend of Mobo, the invincible warrior from another world, began to spread like wildfire. Fear, doubt, but also admiration coursed through the hearts of all who had witnessed this marvel. All media and networks broadcast live images. Justine and Lydia were among the crowd gathered near the pyramid. They were petrified by what they had just seen. Yet Lydia found the courage to hold her phone upright, contributing in her own way to the live coverage of that night which would forever be etched in collective memory. All of humanity had just awakened, physically and spiritually, to witness this foundational event. Some wept, others celebrated. Others calculated the impossibility of the pyramid staying intact in the air. The clever ones sought ways to profit from it. Some called to hire the admiral. Others even planned to kidnap him for ransom or to extract the secret of his power. Yet many across the globe remained silent that night. They were incapable of any reaction in front of what seemed to be a divine apparition.

The close-up of Mobo's face, bloodied and battered, yet radiating indescribable power, remained etched in everyone's memory, a symbol of unparalleled strength and wisdom. The pyramid itself, once again solidly anchored to the ground, became a silent reminder of Mobo's

HER FRIENDS

insurmountable feat and the hope that can arise even in the darkest moments.

The moon had always been an object of fascination for humanity. Its luminous glow in the night sky brought a certain peace and serenity to observers. But that night, everything was about to change. Cameras trained on it revealed a strange and chilling phenomenon. The usual glow had mysteriously vanished, as if a dark force had chosen to cover it with a shroud of darkness. Witnesses let out a collective scream of horror as a massive shadow loomed before the moon, three times its size. The silence that had enveloped the crowd at the sight of this unexpected eclipse was quickly shattered by a murmured wave of concern.

However, it was not just the size of the shadow that terrified the witnesses. It was the vast red lights coursing through that dark silhouette, resembling both threatening eyes and fiery wounds. The brightness of these red lights was so intense that it lit up the night with a sinister glow, creating an eerie and oppressive atmosphere. Faces turned pale, and their wide-open eyes betrayed their sheer terror.

Local authorities were quickly alerted to this strange phenomenon and dispatched experts from various fields in an attempt to explain the unusual eclipse. Scientists, watching the images broadcast by the cameras, were astonished. Questions raced through their minds. What could possibly cause such a massive shadow to cross the sky? And why was this shadow accompanied by red lights, almost demonic?

Yet, despite their years of experience and deep knowledge of the universe, even the most prominent scientists had never witnessed anything like it. They were faced with a mystery they could not solve. Fear slowed their minds. In the frenzy, the most outlandish hypotheses flew in all directions, ranging from unexplained natural phenomena to implausible conspiracy theories.

However, while debates raged among the experts, no one suspected the spacecraft approaching silently from another world. Its presence was unknown to all. Its shape was indecipherable, shrouded in the shadows of eternal night.

The tension mounted as the shadow of the eclipse extended. Experts, scientists, and civilians alike were left wondering what would happen next. And the truth is that no one had a magic button that night to stop the progression of that indescribable thing in the sky. No one?"

HER FRIENDS

Moment of Truth

Great Pyramid, Giza

Sara was about to get into the SUV that had come to pick her up when she sensed an oppressive presence behind her and turned around. The wind swept through Admiral Mobo's black hair, giving his gaze a wild gleam. His entire body was smeared with blood, the multiple assaults he had just endured leaving no mercy. Despite this, his figure remained imposing and threatening. The Martian's driver quickly got out of the vehicle, pointing a laser-sighted automatic rifle at the injured giant. But she stopped him abruptly, gently motioning for him to put his weapon away.

"You're not afraid of me anymore?" Mobo growled, managing a slight smile as he fixed his gaze on her, as if trying to probe her soul.

She stepped closer to him, fascinated by his battered body, wondering how he could still be alive.

"You must be in terrible pain..." she let slip, torn between disgust and compassion.

"Pain is ephemeral," Mobo replied, wiping a trickle of blood from the corner of his mouth with the back of his hand.

"Why are you following me?" she asked, already guessing his answer.

The events she had just experienced had completely destabilized her, putting her on the brink of death multiple times. But she was no longer the arrogant little fool looking for a job. She had seen all her certainties crumble in a new reality—one for which she was in no way prepared. She had dug deep within herself to find the courage she never knew she possessed. The courage to save her fellow beings from a terrible confrontation with visitors from another world. These

HER FRIENDS

"friends," as Kurtz called them with his typical cynical humor. She had quickly realized she could no longer escape this new fate that was hers because she was the key. She was the augmented virus the Martian was going to inject into that rocky, blood-red vessel to destroy it. Each time she thought of this new reality, her mind spiraled, engulfed in vertigo. Yet it was an unshakeable and brutal reality. She knew well that this giant sought to capture her, probably to kill her.

"I must take you back to the Grand Master," Mobo confessed with sadness and firmness.

She challenged him with her gaze and calmly asked, "Do you have to kill me?"

The surprise was immediate and anxiety-ridden for Mobo, who instinctively stepped back a few paces, almost falling over. Regaining his balance with difficulty, he straightened up, blood splattering Sara's face and the windows of the vehicle. The driver pointed his laser rifle again at Mobo's forehead, the tiny red dot settled between his eyes.

"You're following me to kill me, aren't you?" she pressed provocatively.

"Silence!" Mobo commanded, extending his arm toward her, his jaw clenched and barely managing to stifle a hiss from the back of his throat. "Who wants to die?"

She stepped closer to him, feeling his breath and the stench of decay. His face was horrific to behold. Shreds of skin revealed what looked like bolts and machinery beneath. A violent fear gripped her, paralyzing her whole body. But strangely, she managed to control it. She wouldn't give this fear a chance to dominate her.

"You saved my life. Why?" she demanded, lifting her chin proudly to insist on a clear and deserved explanation. Mobo squinted, like a wild beast assessing its prey before pouncing.

"You must live, Sara!" he replied without breaking eye contact.

"It's incredible: everyone wants me to survive in this situation!" she laughed, shrugging and smacking her hands on her thighs. Instinctively, Mobo followed her every movement, not missing a beat.

"I saw you in a dream. And with your mysterious message, I even know your name: MOBO!" she whispered to him.

The admiral seemed pleased with this revelation, leaning slightly toward her, as if to thank her. This gesture was misinterpreted by the driver, who fired a burst of bullets straight into Mobo's forehead. The admiral roared like a wounded animal, stumbling back a few steps and visibly preparing to retaliate violently.

"What are you doing? You fool!" she screamed, disarming the driver and delivering a blow with the rifle's butt that shattered his face.

Admiral Mobo's eyes were now covered in fresh blood, but he didn't lose an ounce of his determination.

She had just defended him.

She returned the rifle to the driver, whom she shoved against the car's body, before taking her position in front of the admiral, as if to apologize.

"You are a slave, Mobo. You're just a pathetic plaything in the claws of your Grand Boss, or whatever he is!" she shot out in a reproachful and humiliating tone.

"The Grand Master sent Struiz to destroy you. And I killed him to save you," Mobo murmured as he straightened up and wiped the blood flowing from his forehead.

"Listen to me carefully. This Struiz has reconstituted himself; I don't know by what magic. He wreaked havoc on our ship, the Merlin, far more than you can imagine. Innocent lives were lost because of his insatiable ambition. Your Grand Master is not the sole bearer of this suffering, but he authorized it. It's time for you to rebel, Mobo," she continued as if finally reading the truth of the intimate struggle that had consumed the admiral for so long.

HER FRIENDS

Mobo's eyes widened as Sara recounted the horrors committed by Struiz, describing each face, every shattered life.

"How can you endure all this? How do you find the strength to continue?" he asked, fascinated by the courage he was beginning to admire.

"Because I refuse to accept cruelty and to be directed by fear. I refuse to be a victim. Mobo, we all have a strength within us, a power your Grand Master cannot control. And that power is the love we have for one another, the desire to protect those we cherish. You have that strength in you, Mobo. Don't waste it. Use it!" she said, barely pausing for breath, as if pleading.

Mobo turned his gaze away with a swift motion. Pain and deep rage were etched on his face. She felt her words starting to penetrate his mind. He screamed, raising his fists toward the ship that hid the moon, beside himself.

"What are you going to do now?" she questioned, her voice heavy with emotion. "Did you see how everyone reacted to your act with that pyramid? How did you lift that mass all by yourself?"

He looked at the pyramid and at Sara. "It was a student project when I was studying at Massala University."

"A student project?" she exclaimed, stunned by the implication that he had already been in contact with humans. "I can't believe it," she continued. Her eyes gazed blankly, as if she were speaking to herself. She understood: this was not his first visit here.

"I'm not asking you to believe."

"Did you see those faces, those people bowing down? And those who began to pray? In mere seconds, you became a living God."

"I did not become one."

"Where are you going?" she asked, seeing him turn his back to flee.

Without stopping in his tracks, he turned his head over his shoulder to look at her one last time. "Kill the Grand Master," he growled in a grave tone, a deep rasp, before disappearing behind the mound.

"Mobo!" she cried, helpless.

She wished this conversation would never end. She felt she had so much to learn, so much to understand about why this improbable being from nowhere was so interested in her insignificant little life among billions of others.

Sara leaned against the hood of the car and let her tears and sobs pour out of her body, like letting the rushing water explode into the river after having held it back for so long. Bloodied jaw, the driver approached her to comfort her and invite her to get inside the cabin.

The vehicle started up and slowly made its way around the heart of this scene of unmatched grandeur. The lucky witnesses who had beheld the majestic pyramid lifted by the incredible strength of Admiral Mobo were now rushing to touch it. They perhaps hoped to absorb a fraction of that inconceivable power. Hearts raced with inexpressible excitement as hands reached out toward the monumental structure.

The crowd, now intoxicated by this extraordinary event, was gripped by an almost mystical feeling. Some knelt before the imposing pyramid, seeing it as a tangible manifestation of a benevolent deity. Their faith was mirrored in silent prayers, whispered softly, enchanting and fervent, as others joined in, filling the air with a religious atmosphere imbued with reverence and devotion.

But amid these acts of piety, the clamor of the crowd often cast a veil of anxiety over the scene. Like tumultuous waves, the movements of the crowd formed and broke with irresistible force, creating moments of scattered panic. Cries and weeping rose up, conveying fear and confusion, as each individual desperately tried to find their place in this shifting sea of adoration.

The law enforcement and army hastily dispatched to the site were themselves caught off guard, caught between spiritual ecstasy and indomitable chaos. Some, spellbound by the divine grandeur and splendor unfolding before their eyes, refused to leave the vicinity of the pyramid, clinging to it like a crutch to fulfill their devotion. Others, however, swept up by the human tide, were caught in a frightening turmoil, desperately seeking to escape this uncontrollable frenzy.

Amidst this chaos, Lydia was devastated by the loss of her mother Justine, who had wandered toward the pyramid, drawn by an irresistible impulse. The image haunting Lydia was that of a woman completely possessed.

Heading to The Martian

The Martian Institute's 4x4 vehicle

"Sara, it's time to proceed with the transfer of your DNA," Kurtz announced in a grave voice.

"Seriously? Now? How does it work? Wi-Fi?" she asked playfully, trying to lighten the mood.

Kurtz managed a smile on the monitor as he replied, "Well, technically, we use a secure line. We take your code, transmit it here to the lab, and print it. It's child's play, you see?"

"Okay. Got it. I won't be surprised by anything anymore," she joked, well aware that the situation was far more serious than he let on.

"We can't afford to wait any longer. We absolutely must neutralize those guys."

"They look pretty tough, though," she pointed out with an impressed pout.

"I have faith. The cannon is ready. Unfortunately, we have less time than we anticipated. Their ship could land on Earth at any moment, and then we'd lose all our chances," Kurtz declared, his voice almost frantic.

Kurtz's alarmed tone secretly amused Sara. She understood the situation well: the world had reached a tipping point. But she doubted anyone could stop these entities from space. Humans seemed far too vulnerable in the face of such a threat. When a single individual could manipulate a pyramid like a toy, what could an entire army of guys like him do? And the size of their ship suggested they were far more numerous than that.

Driving cautiously, Isham, the driver, indicated to Sara where to place her finger for the sample. "Under the red light, once your finger is properly positioned, the light will turn green, and the sample will be taken automatically. You'll only feel a slight pinch from the needle," he explained, glancing at her in the rearview mirror.

"Let's not waste time. Go ahead," Kurtz added impatiently, frowning.

"I'm ready, the light is green," she noted. "Can I take my finger back now?"

"Perfect, let me take a look," Kurtz said in a focused tone. "That's great, super! I need to tell you something..." His voice became calmer, as if he wanted to share a secret. "Without you, we wouldn't have come this far. In a few minutes, the quantum cannon will be ready to fire on that ship and send it back into the void. I just wanted to say one thing: thank you!"

She felt a warmth fill her heart as Kurtz's gratitude touched her deeply. An emotional wave took over, causing her to tear up for a moment.

"You've been incredible," Isham confirmed. She was not used to such recognition.

"I'm not incredible, but I did everything I could," she said, trying to wipe away her tears.

"You already know this, but you've probably just saved the world," Kurtz continued as the sounds of crashes multiplied around him.

"What's happening, Kurtz? Those noises behind you?" she asked, surprised by the intensity of the cacophony.

"Damn it... Don't get too close... Isham, take her to safety..." Kurtz said, his voice filled with panic amid the clashing sounds.

The communication abruptly cut off. Those were Kurtz's last words, swallowed by the turmoil that seemed to be pure chaos.

"Isham, can you call him back?" she asked, her voice trembling.

"The secure connection is broken," Isham replied in a flat tone.

"Then use your phone, I don't know! Did you hear those noises? That wasn't nothing, right?" she exclaimed, mixing worry with amusement. "What exactly is going on?"

HER FRIENDS

"We're taking a detour. We're no longer heading to the Martian base. There's something dangerous over there," Isham declared, trying to convince her with furtive glances in the rearview mirror.

She didn't waste time weighing the consequences of her decision. She was determined to reach the Martian Institute, no matter what. Isham, on the other hand, found himself torn between his duty to protect her and his strong desire to help Kurtz, a long-time friend. Sara's words, spoken in a firm and resolved tone, left no room for discussion.

"Isham, we're going to the Martian Institute," she stated without hesitation.

A silence settled in the car as Isham weighed the pros and cons. Stick to the protocol established for years in situations like this, or listen to his instinct and support her in her rescue mission. The road stretched out before them, and Isham lost himself in thought.

After a long moment of reflection, he finally looked up and met her gaze, still laced with apprehension.

"You're brave and strong; I can't deny that," he began solemnly. "But the situation is extremely dangerous. I can't let you take such a risk, not without a solid strategy."

Surprisingly calm, she firmly replied "NO," shaking her head from left to right. She understood Isham's concerns but was convinced that the urgency of the situation required immediate and effective action.

"Isham, honestly, do you think we have time for strategy? Kurtz is in deep trouble. We're going in and getting him!" she snapped in a serious, almost threatening tone. "He needs our help, and I refuse to sit back while things get worse."

Isham felt the intensity of Sara's determination fill the car. He knew he could no longer back down; he couldn't abandon his friend at this crucial moment. Ultimately, he nodded.

"Alright, let's head to the Martian Institute," he said energetically. "But first, change your clothes. And I need to talk to you about your new powers."

She fixed him with a stare in the rearview mirror, looking at him as if he were drunk.

"You'll see. Pull on the handle on the floor under your feet and put on these clothes," he advised, a small smile playing on his lips.

"What are these things? Are we going to the gym?" she joked, discovering a complete sports outfit.

Isham looked at Sara with a mix of admiration and concern in his eyes. He knew he had to put aside his own fears and apprehensions and tell her what he knew. He took a deep breath before starting his story.

"You'll be more comfortable for the fight in those clothes," he said, carefully choosing his words. He didn't want to scare her or overwhelm her with too much information. "But there's something you need to know. Something disconcerting."

She gazed into Isham's eyes, eager to learn what troubled him so much. "What fight?" she asked, her voice calm but curious.

Isham took a deep breath before continuing. "Your DNA has undergone a mutation," he explained calmly. "Your entire body has been transformed into something... else."

Instinctively, her eyes widened as she tried to grasp the gravity of his words. "Wait, what's this nonsense?" she asked incredulously.

Isham swallowed hard before responding. "Yes, exactly," he said in a low voice. "And this transformation has given you superhuman strength. I don't know more. But I know it's huge."

"Got it. I understand! Am I your strategy? Is that it?" she asked teasingly.

Isham nodded, a soft smile on his lips. "It's possible. But you'll need to learn to control it. This isn't something to take lightly," he continued, still holding his sore jaw.

HER FRIENDS

She looked at him with the wide-eyed wonder of a child dreaming: "I'm no longer afraid to improvise," she said calmly. "And I need to save Kurtz. They've already hurt us enough. I'll do what it takes."

"I trust you," he said softly as she changed.

"Are you okay, do you like me?" she asked as she stared at him in the rearview mirror. He smiled, looking away.

After removing her suit and putting on her new clothes, she incredulously noticed that her scar around her waist was gone.

"Isham! Look! My scar is gone!" she exclaimed, realizing she no longer needed her space suit to stand upright. She could walk again, all by herself.

PAUL TOSKIAM

Where are you going, Mom?

Giza, Egypt

Justine and her daughter Lydia struggled to make their way through the dense crowd pressing around the pyramid. The stifling heat seemed to amplify the surrounding commotion, as people jostled them from all sides in indescribable chaos.

"Lydia, stay close to me!" Justine shouted over the din. She grabbed her daughter's hand firmly to prevent her from being swept away by the throng.

Lydia, her eyes wide with momentary panic, tried to dodge the unintentional bumps from people crossing in all directions.

"Where are we going, Mom?" she yelled, being pulled along forcefully by her mother.

"We're heading towards him!" Justine shouted, pointing to a bike that was leaning against a nearby wall. Miraculously, the bike had been spared by the dense crowd and seemed to have been placed there for them.

Without thinking twice, Justine seized it and told her daughter, "Lydia, get on behind me! We need to hurry."

Lydia was increasingly confused about where her mom was taking them. Until now, she had just focused on keeping her in sight and was now simply following her instructions.

Justine and Lydia mounted the bike, but they still had to fight their way through the thick crowd. Pedestrians swarmed around them, some casting irritated glances, while others shouted for them to be careful. Lydia, sitting at the back, rolled her eyes dramatically and mimicked the shouts of passerby. Her mother couldn't help but laugh despite the tense situation.

"Mom, you're such an adventurer tonight!" Lydia declared with a mischievous smile.

Justine, focused on the path ahead, replied laughing, "I don't know exactly where we're going, but we're going! Hold on tight!"

They turned into a narrow street where the crowd was less dense to gradually distance themselves from the city. As they rode towards the unknown, the warm desert wind whipped across their faces. The murmurs of tourists and locals gradually faded, and the sounds of honking and the city's usual clamor receded. All that remained was the gentle whistling of the wind and the steady hum of the bike's tires.

"Mom, seriously, where are we going?" Lydia asked curiously.

"Just a feeling, my dear. As if the desert has something to tell us," Justine replied, her gaze lost in the distance. Lydia, trusting her mother, tightened her embrace around her waist. The two women moved forward, propelled by an invisible force.

HER FRIENDS

The Dock--------The Martian Institute's premises

"You could almost film a horror movie in this corner!" Sara joked as she approached the entrance ramp.

"You've kept your humor intact," Isham pointed out.

"I've died several times already. I fear nothing anymore," she replied, spinning around to test the flexibility of her sportswear. "This material is great. I really like it. What is it?"

Isham waved his hand to signal her to stop talking. The entrance gate at the bottom of the descending ramp had just started to open.

"Is someone there?" she whispered, not taking her eyes off the gate.

Isham shrugged to indicate he didn't know and placed his index finger in front of his lips to ask for silence. He activated a small terminal attached to his equipment. He nervously scanned various screens that resembled images from security cameras, zooming in on some to better assess the details. He waited a few seconds, staring at the gate before sitting down impassively.

She grabbed the terminal from him and glanced at the images showing rooms strewn with corpses, drenched in a shocking pool of blood.

"Damn it, Isham, what's all this blood?" she asked, horrified.

"There's something terrible in there..." he confided, his gaze hollow as he realized that all his colleagues at The Martian had just been brutally slaughtered.

Taking a deep breath, he stood up from his crouched position and readied his machine gun. He was armed like a one-man regiment: two automatic rifles, four handguns, cross-straps of ammunition across his chest, and shark knives. All that gear must weigh a ton. She felt a twinge of jealousy since he hadn't offered her any of those toys. From that perspective, she felt almost naked.

HER FRIENDS

Still crouched in commando mode, Isham signaled her to follow as they moved along the wall down toward the gate.

This wide ramp, designed to accommodate all kinds of vehicles, opened like a rectangular hole in the sandy plain. It led to the loading dock of The Martian.

This was certainly not the type of place people stumbled upon by accident. And that night, with nothing but the lights of another world shining before the moon, the reddish ambiance was particularly grim.

Feeling somewhat audacious and confident, Sara broke the silence with another touch of biting humor. "I can totally see a story featuring zombie-cannibal mummies or something like that!" she joked, slowly approaching the entrance ramp. Her words, imbued with feigned lightness, contrasted sharply with the heavy atmosphere enveloping the place.

Isham displayed an impassive resolution. "When you see one, try not to scream too loud!" he teased her, amused.

Running her fingertips over the soft fabric of her sports clothes, she executed a graceful pirouette. "I've died several times already. I fear nothing." Her words seemed to come from a previous life, from a time so recent yet already distant in her mind, when she lived an ordinary life that she did not regret.

Isham, seasoned and silent, gestured for her to be quiet. The creaking of the entrance gate, under the influence of some invisible force, broke the silence of the night. The faint glow of their flashlights flickered as a whispering voice seemed to escape from the void.

"Who is it?" she whispered, her eyes glued to the dark opening of the gate, suddenly feeling less reassured.

Isham, a man of few words, shrugged in uncertainty as he readied his machine gun with meticulous precision. He had equipped himself like a mobile fortress: two automatic rifles, four handguns, two cross-straps of ammunition across his chest, and sharp knives reminiscent of shark teeth. Sara, looking at his arsenal with a twinge of jealousy, felt vulnerable, slightly naked without any gear.

Isham crouched and slipped into commando position. His movements became fluid and silent. With an imperceptible gesture, he signaled for her to follow, skirting the wall down toward the gaping gate. Their shadows blended into the night, becoming an indistinct part of the surrounding darkness. They stood ready to face whatever lurked behind that half-open gate. Even if it was very ugly.

They leaned to pass through the slight opening of the gate and stepped into the vast hidden dock of The Martian.

Their silent steps echoed softly on the concrete floor stretching out before them. As they cautiously advanced into the vastness of the hangar, the sounds of chains clanking against metal filled the muffled air. They exchanged glances, their eyes reflecting the horror emanating from the shadows.

Soon, they reached the back of the hangar, where the source of those sinister noises resided.

Illuminating ahead with their flashlights, they were gripped by terror. The bodies of Kurtz and Admiral Mobo dangled before them. They were suspended by chains from their arms, their bodies severed at the waist. Streams of blood still flowed along their dangling entrails. Kurtz was motionless, but Mobo appeared to be still alive.

Sara was about to scream to expel the fear and visceral horror that had just overwhelmed her, but Isham forcefully covered her mouth.

Gathering her courage, she approached Kurtz and stared at him while plugging her nose to keep from throwing up. His face oddly retained an expression of inner peace despite the brutal execution. Poor Kurtz. Fate had robbed him of the joy of seeing his mission accomplished. She recalled her father George's words, a great optimist but also depressed, repeated endlessly: "Live every second as if it's your last." He was right, the old man.

HER FRIENDS

Feeling her presence, Admiral Mobo suddenly opened his eyes and looked at her with infinite sadness in his black eyes, where the light from their flashlights danced. He groaned in pain, a deep rattle causing abundant streams of blood to flow from his entrails to the ground. This Mobo was more human than he appeared. She asked him, her voice filled with restrained anger: "Who did this, Mobo?" He lifted his eyes and looked ahead, articulating something incomprehensible, exerting extreme effort at that moment.

Sensing movement behind them, they turned around very slowly, with great caution.

Before them stood a huge, viscous figure, writhing and undulating in inhuman spasms. Gelatinous tentacles emerged from its misshapen body, pulsating as if animated by their own will.

Sara felt her legs give way as her breath caught in her throat. Isham was frozen, his weapon forgotten in his trembling hands. This creature, this abomination, defied all logic and seemed to emerge straight from a nightmare.

The monster's gaze fixed upon them, its pupil-less eyes shooting malevolent green sparks. A powerful, insane rage emanated from this deformed being. It reared up and flung the lower halves of Kurtz and Admiral Mobo's bodies into the air, which landed at their feet.

"Here's what happens to traitors!" growled the creature as it began to advance toward them menacingly.

Seeing the dismembered bodies lying at its feet, Isham was overcome with panic and rage. Having remained silent on the sidelines, he became caught in the whirlwind of a powerful adrenaline rush. He readied both of his automatic rifles with a swift gesture and began to unleash bullets at the living form before him. He screamed like a madman to control the recoil of his weapons.

The creature emitted a multitude of high-pitched screams. Suddenly quick as a flash, it began zigzagging and bouncing off the walls to evade the bullets. Isham kept his aim and pivoted as much as necessary to never miss his target. The cartridges flew by, and Sara helped him reload.

Isham froze again; he couldn't pull his gaze away from the bodies lying on the ground. He was battling against the panic that tried to paralyze him. He had seen horrible things in his life, yet never anything like this.

He shook his head rapidly, as if trying to wake from a nightmare, and lunged at the enemy. He readied both of his automatic rifles and began firing. Bullets flew, cutting trough the creature's flesh. It screeched again, but did not stop.

The creature was fast and unpredictable. It dodged the bullets with unsettling ease. Isham was beginning to lose hope.

Suddenly, the creature leapt towards him. Isham barely had time to dive aside to avoid being flattened. The creature passed through him, leaving a trail of blood and flesh behind.

Isham stood up, completely soaked in the stinking, slimy substance, but ready to continue the fight. But the creature had already vanished. It had evaporated into the darkness.

They were exhausted and in shock. They had survived a traumatic experience.

"If you planned to take a shower, now's the time!" she joked to relieve the nervous tension and celebrate the simple fact that they were still alive.

"It's sweet; he must be diabetic!" Isham retorted, spitting out a mouthful of that flabby gelatin with a grimace of disgust.

Sara approached Mobo, her throat tight. Despite the revulsion his shredded body invoked in her, she reached out to touch him. She didn't forget that this warrior had saved her life. You don't forget those who save your life.

Mobo's skin was cold and clammy. His long black hair was matted, almost braided around his exposed entrails. She could smell the blood and death that surrounded them.

HER FRIENDS

"Is he your Grand Master?" she asked in a trembling voice.

Mobo blinked despairingly. With a grimace of pain and a wheeze from his lungs, he indicated that he would return. Then he closed his eyes, lowering his head, dazzled by the bright light that Isham had just turned back on.

A wave of heavy emotions washed over her. She was terrified, yet also in awe of Mobo's strength and courage. It wasn't the right moment, but she also felt drawn to him, captivated by his wild beauty and vulnerability.

"Help me, we will detach them!" she asked Isham. "Let's hurry. He will be back."

"I gave him a good dose!" he boasted as he fired short bursts at the chains of the two unfortunate people hanging there, who fell to the ground like chunks of meat in their blood.

She approached Mobo and placed her hand on his shoulder. He was so tall and strong, yet he seemed so fragile. She bent down to help him up and was surprised to find she could easily move this body that was twice her size. She glanced at Isham. He didn't seem surprised.

"Did you see that?" she asked him.

Isham smiled. "Just a little," he said.

Sara and Isham locked eyes, like two veterans ready for a second round that didn't take long to come.

The Grand Master appeared once again before them, playing with his imposing and threatening silhouette. He had taken on a more human appearance, but he was still at least twice the size of Admiral Mobo.

With a thunderous crash, the Grand Master suddenly emerged, like a giant rising from the darkness. He was two times larger than Admiral Mobo, and his formidable figure was clad in strange and brutal armor.

The armor, made of black and shiny metal adorned with geometric patterns and strange runes, moved with him like a second skin. Dotted with blades and spikes, it exuded an aura of threat so intense that it made the bravest hearts tremble.

The Grand Master's muscles bulged and tensed, impressive, sculpted by years of fierce combat. Each of his movements hinted at that animalistic power beneath his armor, ready to spring into action.

A warrior's headdress made of prehistoric bird feathers crowned his head defiantly. The giant feathers gleamed a deep black and floated in the air like flames with each movement.

The Grand Master displayed, unmistakably, a blend of raw power and aerial agility. He was the leader of the invading army, descended personally to retrieve what he had come for, which none of his closest admirals had managed to bring him. His anger was matched only by his desire to acquire a sample of Sara's DNA.

However, Isham was not intimidated by this change in form. He proved to be a formidable fighter, and Sara's admiration for him only grew. He merely reloaded his rifles and walked toward him, determined to end it. Without a second of hesitation, she followed him, her heart racing like a war drum.

Her whole body urged her to flee to protect herself from this monster ready to tear them apart. But she hadn't come this far for nothing or by chance.

If her body wanted nothing more than to escape, her mind was focused on a single idea, clear, simple, and powerful: to destroy the Grand Master.

Her desire had grown larger than herself. This was no longer about fulfilling a personal whim, but about completing a mission, righting a wrong, saving lives.

She wanted this for Kurtz, who had died for his ideals. She wanted his sacrifice to not be in vain. That it would serve to change the world and push back those space maniacs with their brutal power delusions.

HER FRIENDS

She wanted it for her Martian companions, who had perished too soon. She wanted their deaths not to be pointless, that they hadn't given their lives in vain.

She wanted it for her father, who had never truly understood her. His illness and fear of the nearing end had softened him. But deep down, he had never really regarded her. She too had her share of responsibility; having locked herself in a selfish life. She wanted to prove to him that she could also surpass herself, as an adult, and that she was worthy of his recognition, of his love.

And she wanted it for Earth, whose fate seemed insignificant to her just a few hours ago. Those intruders from elsewhere had given her the insight: Earth was so fragile, like a chick before a wolf's jaws.

Their moment of truth had come.

She felt liberated, finally. For years, she had been a prisoner of her fears, doubts, and inhibitions. This moment had allowed her to cross that invisible and burdensome barrier. Now, she had no mental brakes.

She had learned to master her emotions, to control her mind. She was ready to face the Grand Master, with a new feeling, the belief that she could defeat him, even if she didn't know how.

The Grand Master did not move and Isham had already emptied several magazines into him.

The bullets ricocheted off his body like flies on a window. The Grand Master was invulnerable.

With a motion of his entire body, as if he were returning a two-handed tennis shot, the Grand Master hurled Isham against the wall at a dizzying speed.

Isham soared halfway across the dock and crashed into the wall with absolute violence. He exploded like a balloon filled with liquid, his weapons crashing to the ground as the remnants of his body slowly dripped down the wall.

Sara shut her eyes, horrified. She had just witnessed her companion die before her in a horrendous manner.

"There's no point in resisting, miserable creature!"

The Grand Master's voice thundered in the dock, like a clap of thunder. It reverberated through the walls and chains, as if he were speaking into a powerful concert sound system.

A grimace of pain crossed her face as she covered her ears with her fingers instinctively shutting her eyes.

When she opened her eyes again, she locked onto the dark gaze of the Grand Master advancing toward her like an unstoppable fate, a cruel and satisfied smile on his face.

The Grand Master struck first with a swift and powerful movement. His fists swept through the air with incredible force, creating shockwaves that shook the ground deeply. And it was no small detail, as the place was buried below ground. This power was prodigious, akin to an earthquake. Sara instinctively dodged each strike, moving with graceful agility and broad movements allowed by her outfit.

"You cannot defeat me, Sara," said the Grand Master in a cold, cavernous voice. "I am far beyond your comprehension."

She did not respond. She thought to herself that, for a high dignitary of an extraterrestrial race, he was sorely lacking in conversation. He sounded like a crude automated character from a video game spouting his lines without soul. And it was precisely this that made him as despicable as he was formidable: this absence of any form of empathy. He was a space psychopath, here to slaughter her, like all the others, and to retrieve her DNA. This grim idea gave her a new impulse.

She focused solely on the movements of her opponent, to evade them. She could not afford to be distracted. Each blow from the Grand Master seemed unpredictable and could be lethal. But she began to read his movements with a clarity that astonished her. She dodged, blocked, and countered each attack with deadly precision. No human would have survived. But the Grand Master held his ground.

HER FRIENDS

At times, their bodies danced within the hangar, moving almost in harmony. The walls trembled under the brute force of their movements. Each strike was delivered with unparalleled vehemence as both fought for their survival.

As the battle raged on, Sara began to tire. The Grand Master's powerful blows inflicted deep wounds, but she held on, refusing to yield to the pain. She no longer wished to retreat. She still saw only one way out: the death of this monster.

"You cannot defeat me, human," growled the Grand Master, sweeping his arm in a wide gesture.

She nimbly dodged the attack, but was caught off guard when the Grand Master lunged at her with astonishing speed. He grabbed her arm and threw her violently to the ground. He seized her again and hurled her down once more, with increased force. The second impact knocked the breath out of her and she felt bursts of pain shoot through every part of her body.

She refused to be broken. She rose again, summoning all her courage. Her mind tapped into a strength she didn't know existed, a force coming from far beyond her own being.

"I will break you," she said, her voice filled with rage.

Sara delivered every strike with brutal intensity. She had seen Mobo do it at the foot of the Eiffel Tower. She struck to kill. She utilized every movement to her advantage, exploiting her opponent's reflexes and power against him.

Soon, she found an opening. Using all her strength, she delivered a precise kick to the Grand Master's knee, making him buckle. She followed up with a powerful uppercut straight to his chin, forcing his head back.

The Grand Master staggered but did not fall. Instead, he straightened up, his face twisting into a sadistic grin. He seemed to revel in the pain, feeding off his own suffering.

She took a deep breath and launched into one final assault. She struck with surprising velocity, her fists and legs moving with surgical precision. The Grand Master tried to retaliate, but each blow was either blocked or dodged with ease.

Finally, she executed a powerful roundhouse kick to the Grand Master's torso, sending him crashing violently against the wall in another shockwave that made the dock tremble.

She thought she had defeated the brainless brute in this clash that resembled a sad street fight. But her enemy was more devious than he appeared.

With a flick of his hand, he released a swarm of small black orbs that sped across the ground. They seized her by the feet and swept her off her feet in a vertiginous fall. Her skull hit the ground with a deafening crash.

The orbs wrapped around her like the casing of a sausage and lifted her into the air, hovering. She was powerless, suspended like a piece of meat at the mercy of her enemy.

Dazed and disoriented, she locked eyes with Admiral Mobo. That brave man was still there, ready to fight by her side, forgetting that he was completely torn apart. He had no strength left. Sara's heart broke at the sight of her fallen space knight.

At that moment, a flashback struck her: "...you're not here by chance. The ship we have in front of us is what we call a super predator...", the words of the unfortunate Dr. Carlo Mancini echoed in her mind. She understood what Carlo meant by "Super Predator." The Grand Master had only sown death and despair.

Apparently, it wasn't an exclusive human phenomenon: the entire universe seemed infested with malevolent beings.

Why did the universe insist on creating these killing machines?

Why was death his centerpiece, his ultimate invention?

Floating in the air, powerless, suspended like a mere piece of meat, Sara expected to encounter this masterpiece of the universe: death.

HER FRIENDS

The Grand Master, in his sadistic irreparability, advanced slowly towards her, savoring every second, pushing her to reach the maximum fear a human could endure. His DNA would only benefit from it.

"Where did you learn to hit like that?" the Grand Master asked, close enough for Sara to feel his breath, sniffing her as if intoxicated by the scent of her skin.

Her skin smelled of jasmine, fresh and delicate, like a spring morning.

The Grand Master inhaled deeply, the scent of Sara filling his lungs. He was fascinated by her, by her strength and beauty. He cast his wild eyes sideways at the remains of Admiral Mobo.

"You were right, old fellow: she is delectable!" he growled, bursting into a powerful, acoustic laughter while caressing Sara's face with the tips of his claws.

"Don't touch me, you little piece of shit!" she shot back, tired of his antics and no longer afraid of the consequences.

"One does not speak to the Grand Master that way without facing his wrath," he declared, piercing Sara's chest with calculated slowness. First, his claws, then his entire fingers dove in effortlessly. They tore through Sara's flesh, grinding her bones one by one until they cracked. She screamed until it felt like her veins would explode. He was maniacally digging a blood-filled orifice, growing wider and deeper until he penetrated through her entire body.

She was overtaken by violent spasms that shook her frantically in the air. She screamed in agony, but the Grand Master didn't even look at her, too absorbed in his task. Even when his face was splattered repeatedly with jets of blood as he severed the heart's arteries. He remained imperturbably focused, like one accustomed to performing these surgeries without anesthesia.

Soon the Grand Master's body fell victim to a series of spasms, accompanied by flashes of light swirling around him. He had obtained what he had come for. He had traveled in person all the way from the depths of the galaxy. Above all, he craved the unique power boost contained in the DNA of this human.

"Too easy!" he murmured to himself, withdrawing his arm from Sara's entrails. He shook his arm and pressed toward the dock exit to reach his ship and leave the place after fulfilling his promise: to destroy this insignificant planet that had become useless.

HER FRIENDS

The weapon is born

The Martian Institute's premises

"Mama!" Lydia screamed as she saw her mother slip and roll down the ramp leading to The Martian's dock.

Covered in scratches on her knees and hands, Justine stood up, not paying attention to her pain. She signaled to Lydia to join her without falling like she did. But she immediately changed her mind.

"No! Stay where you are!" Justine suddenly commanded, overcome with nausea as she discovered the carnage that had taken place in this huge, cold, and gloomy dock.

"What's wrong, Mama?" Lydia asked anxiously.

"I'm going to check. Stay here. Wait for me."

"Mama, I'm too scared!"

"DON'T MOVE FROM THERE!" Justine ordered again, wanting to spare her daughter from this dreadful sight. "Hide to the side, and don't look!"

Justine moved forward with the caution of someone entering unknown territory. The smell of blood was extremely strong and almost unbearable. She approached the mangled corpses, observing them with visceral disgust.

What had happened in this place? What could have been at stake for the outcome of this event to be so horrific? Questions flooded Justine's mind. Something she would likely never be able to explain had driven her here. She wasn't crazy. There had to be a reason, a big reason.

Yet, more than ever, she wondered what she was doing there.

Suddenly, she heard a movement behind her. She turned abruptly and saw the remnants of Admiral Mobo looking at her. He lay on the ground, his body bloodied and torn apart. But his eyes were still open, and he was pointing his right hand towards Sara.

Justine took a step back, frightened. She didn't know what the admiral meant.

HER FRIENDS

"What do you want?" she asked, surprised.

Mobo did not respond. He continued to stare at her, his eyes unmoving.

Justine felt a wave of panic wash over her. She turned around and discovered Sara with horror. She was hanging in the air, her head tilted back, her eyes closed.

Justine didn't know what was happening. She tried to move closer to Sara, but she was stopped by an invisible force.

Admiral Mobo continued to point his right hand at Sara.

"SPEAK!" Justine yelled at Mobo.

Admiral Mobo did not move. He kept looking at Sara, exhausted.

Justine felt desperate. She didn't know what to do.

Suddenly, Admiral Mobo spoke.

"Touch her," he said. "Touch her!"

Justine hesitated. "NO!" she screamed towards Lydia, who pretended to move into the dock. She didn't understand what the admiral meant, looking at him in confusion.

"But..." she murmured.

"Touch her," Admiral Mobo repeated. "It's the only way."

Justine took a deep breath. Without fully realizing it, her entire being understood that this half-corpse knew why she had come to this place. It knew her purpose here, at this hour.

She approached Sara with apprehension. Timidly, she placed her hand on her left foot, suspended in the air.

"MAMA!" Lydia screamed as she ran towards her mother, who had just been thrown back several meters by a swirling light of all colors, sparkling as if a sword struck metal.

Sara was still suspended in the air, but her eyes were open. She looked at Justine, a smile on her lips.

"You did it," she said, spitting blood.

Justine still didn't understand the intricacies, too shocked even to listen.

"What happened?" she asked.

"You freed my power," Sara replied. "You gave me the chance to defeat the enemy."

Lydia threw herself into her mother's arms, seeking the comfort she desperately needed at that moment.

"Mama!" Lydia cried out, her voice filled with dread as she watched Justine slip and tumble down the ramp leading to the sinister The Martian's dock.

Justine, covered in wounds on her knees and hands, stood up with fierce determination, ignoring the pain that gnawed at her. With a commanding gesture, she signaled Lydia to join her but hesitated again.

"No! Stay where you are!" Justine suddenly ordered, her face pale from discovering the horror that reigned over this vast, cold, and dark dock.

"What happened, Mama?" Lydia asked, terror gripping her.

"I'm going to check. Stay here. Wait for me."

"Mama, I'm so scared!"

"DON'T MOVE!" Justine insisted, eager to protect her daughter from the abominations littering the ground. "Hide to the side and don't look!"

With the caution of an explorer in unknown lands, Justine advanced toward the unbearable smell of blood. The mangled corpses lay before her, and she observed them with visceral repulsion.

What drama could have played out here? What colossal stakes could have led to such a tragedy? Questions rushed through Justine's mind. An irresistible force had driven her here, an imperative reason that she could not grasp.

However, at that moment, she felt more lost than ever. Suddenly, a noise behind her made her jump. She turned abruptly and discovered the remnants of Admiral Mobo, his gaze fixed on her. He lay bloody and mutilated, but his eyes were still open, his right hand pointing towards Sara.

HER FRIENDS

A shiver of fear ran through Justine. She did not understand the admiral's intentions.

"What do you want?" she asked, her surprise tinged with worry.

Mobo remained silent, his gaze never leaving Sara, as if he had locked onto her at the center of a target.

Panic seized Justine. She turned towards Sara, suspended in the air, her head tilted back and eyes closed. An invisible force prevented her from getting closer.

Admiral Mobo continued to point his hand at Sara.

"SPEAK!" Justine yelled at Mobo.

Admiral Mobo, impassive and exhausted, continued to observe Sara.

Dismay engulfed Justine. She was lost.

Suddenly, Admiral Mobo spoke.

"Touch her," he articulated. "Touch her!"

Justine hesitated. "NO!" she cried towards Lydia, who was trying to approach the dock. The admiral's intentions were unclear, and she looked at him, bewildered.

"But..." she murmured.

"Touch her," Admiral Mobo repeated. "It's the only way."

Justine breathed deeply. She instinctively understood that this half-corpse knew why she had come to this cursed place. He understood her mission, the purpose that had guided her here. She wasn't crazy. There had to be a reason, a reason of utmost importance.

She approached Sara, her trembling hand brushing against her left foot suspended in the air.

"MAMA!" Lydia screamed as she rushed towards Justine. A swirling light, shimmering in a thousand colors and sparkling like a steel blade, shooting sparks, propelled her back several meters.

Sara remained suspended, eyes open, a smile on her lips.

"You did it," she articulated, spitting blood.

Justine was bewildered. She did not understand: "What happened?" she asked.

"You freed my power. You completed my transformation," Sara replied in a surge of regained energy. "You gave me the chance to save you," she concluded, remembering that she would also save the world, as Kurtz loved to say.

Lydia rushed into her mother's arms, seeking the comfort she desperately needed at that moment.

Justine stroked her daughter's hair as she nestled against her chest. Stunned, she gazed at Sara, who was detaching from her bonds and landing on the ground after a short levitation. Meanwhile, Admiral Mobo was reforming in a transformation marked by the sounds of breaking bones and flesh.

Justine stroked her daughter's hair as she nestled against her chest. Stunned, she gazed at Sara, who was detaching from her bonds and landing on the ground after a short levitation. Meanwhile, Admiral Mobo was reforming in a transformation marked by the sounds of breaking bones and flesh.

In a gesture of maternal love, Justine held her daughter close. She was in awe of what she saw. Sara was alive, and she was free.

Admiral Mobo was back. He was more powerful than ever and roared with rage as if to release an inner tension he wanted to get rid of. It was a matter of mental hygiene.

"THE CANNON!" Kurtz screamed, coming back to himself, still floundering in his own insides and discovering Sara, alive. "The cannon!" he repeated weakly.

She approached him to complete his reconstruction and said these soothing words: "We're going to sort this out in person, once and for all."

Kurtz, still dazed, returned a calm smile before losing consciousness. He didn't have the natural strength of a Mobo within him to withstand the shock of reconstruction. He would need more

HER FRIENDS

time to recover. She was filled with intense joy at the thought of delivering this victory to Kurtz. He wanted it at the cost of his life.

She moved closer to Justine and Lydia, wrapping them in her arms. The incandescent yellow light emanating from her enveloped them like a magical, shimmering cloak.

"The admiral Mobo and I have one last mission to accomplish. I entrust Kurtz to you. Take care of him."

Justine returned a grateful smile, even though she was unable to understand what was really going on. Deep down, she didn't really care. She was so happy to have found and fulfilled her purpose in this life. It goes without saying that Lydia couldn't take her eyes off her. For the first time in her teenage life, she looked at her mother as a heroine, which was a kind of ultimate peak in her value system.

Sara blew them a kiss with both hands, then she dove into the arms of Admiral Mobo. They immediately disappeared as if they had merged into the very air, in a breath that made the walls of the dock tremble down to their foundations.

The place still reeked of death, but for once in the universe, life had just said: NO!

PAUL TOSKIAM

Once upon a time... The Grand Master

Flagship

In the majestic council chamber, the walls were adorned with detailed frescoes depicting the great battles throughout the history of the galaxy. Marble columns rose proudly all around, as if to support the ceiling of a richly decorated temple filled with gold and gemstones. An imposing bay window ran along one side of the room, offering a breathtaking view of Earth, a planet of stunning beauty.

The Grand Master stood on a short dais overlooking the rest of the council. He had donned his sparkling armor, embellished with intricate patterns and shimmering jewels. His face had regained its natural harshness, with deep, powerful features. His war scepter, a symbol of his unquestionable authority, awaited him at his side.

Mission accomplished, he ordered the destruction of Earth and the heading toward his next colony. Earth had brought him nothing but trouble and disappointment. However, the council had a very different scenario in mind.

The Grand Master's voice echoed like a current of air winding its way into every corner.

At the back of the vast chamber emerged the silhouettes of Sara and Admiral Mobo, backlit.

Sara stepped forward toward the Grand Master. She wore a deep blue gown that contrasted with her pale skin. Her long dark hair, braided elegantly, accentuated her graceful silhouette. The fabric shimmered subtly under the ambient light, creating a mysterious aura around her. Threads of electric blue light sparkled along her arms, providing a striking contrast to the rest of her outfit. These almost organic glowing patterns changed color in cycles, creating a hypnotic dance.

Her footsteps resonated, like the echo of a new melody woven with grace. Every detail of the chamber seemed to fade away, leaving only their two gazes locked in a fiery challenge. "You can't do that," she said, pointing towards Earth below the vast bay window, its vibrant blue glow alive with life. "Earth is our home, and we will not let you destroy it."

The Grand Master let out a sarcastic laugh. "You understand nothing, human," he said condescendingly. "I am the one who has conquered entire worlds, who has crushed all resistance in my path. Nothing can stop me."

He crossed his arms, revealing numerous adornments on his attire, each representing a conquered world. His expression conveyed a mix of disdain and arrogant satisfaction. Then he advanced toward her, narrowing his eyes into slits, with contempt and pity. "Fool!" he declared. "I am the Grand Master, and I have decided what happens to you for millennia. Pitiful, insignificant creatures," he finished with a dismissive wave of his hand. Sara held his gaze, fiercer than ever.

Admiral Mobo also stepped forward. Dressed in his immaculate white military uniform and golden epaulettes, he exuded an air of indomitable strength. His face was marked by countless scars, a reminder to all of the battles he had survived.

"You are no longer the Grand Master," he said in a grave voice. "You have lost our trust... irreversibly," he concluded, raising his clenched fist.

The Grand Master's predatory laughter rang out. "I'm pleased to see you intact, Mobo. Have you come to beg for your second punishment?" he mocked, violently throwing two massive daggers before him: one towards Sara, another towards Mobo.

The two weapons whistled through the air, racing across part of the chamber until the council members halted them, shattering them on

HER FRIENDS

the ground into multiple shards. The sound of those daggers hitting the floor marked the Grand Master's fate.

The council members rose from their seats. Their draped robes in dark fabrics seemed to absorb the light of the grand chamber, moving with elegance and majesty. Some were dressed in dark gowns, others in more colorful ones, but all were cloaked in an aura of wisdom and power.

An oppressive silence descended as council members formed a menacing arc around the Grand Master. They exchanged brief glances, silently agreeing on a plan. The air was electric, charged with palpable tension.

The Grand Master found himself surrounded, unable to advance. This was the first time he had seen the council members up close. A new anxiety showed in his eyes as he observed their faces usually hidden in the shadows of their hoods.

As he turned his dazzling armor in a twisting motion, he grasped his scepter, which had until now been integrated into the back of his throne. An electric shiver ran through the chamber as fiery flames erupted from his weapon, creating a burning halo that cast dancing shadows on the chamber walls. The flames seemed to have a life of their own, like serpents poised to strike.

"Traitors!" roared the Grand Master, his thunderous voice echoing like a rumble of thunder. "How dare you defy me? I have delivered half the galaxy to you, without you lifting a finger!"

The councilors remained silent, their faces impassive.

In a flash of fury, he unleashed a storm of fire and wrath. Flaming orbs swirled around him, illuminating the chamber with a demonic glow as they passed. The councilors did not flinch. In a moment of dread, he realized that his magic, once powerful and destructive, seemed to have lost its strength. The dancing flames extinguished, leaving the Grand Master powerless before their united front.

Cornered, he slowly lowered his scepter, his flames dying down. Doubt and worry were evident in his eyes as he looked at the faces of the council members. "Traitors!" he repeated under his breath. "Was the human merely bait?" he muttered, his eyes becoming two horizontal lines, like blades ready to slice.

Unfazed, the councilors invoked their own power, their eyes burning with a mystical glow. A mysterious and powerful energy accumulated around them, forming a strange aura directed at the Grand Master.

In a last-ditch effort, the Grand Master called his elite guard for assistance. Loyal warriors in dark, imposing armor rushed in, prepared to sacrifice themselves for their leader's protection. They had fought alongside him in countless battles, but this time, their loyalty was being tested.

Instead of fighting alongside the Grand Master, they turned against him. Following the council's orders, they positioned themselves between the Grand Master and the councilors, forming an insurmountable barrier.

Incredulous, the Grand Master stared at them, his anger morphing into confusion and pain. He expected his soldiers to stand by him, ready to give their lives for him. But this time, they obeyed a greater power, a power that had recognized the true nature of the Grand Master.

He glared at them, leaning closer to each of them, trying to make them tremble, mulling over the punishment he would inflict. "Traitors! You too?" he whispered, doubt creeping into his mind.

The tension reached its peak. Surrounded by the betrayal of those he had trusted, he felt an all-consuming rage begin to devour him. Slowly, he lowered his scepter, allowing the flames to extinguish completely, realizing that his situation was becoming desperate.

The council's elder, a venerable man with a face marked by the trials of time, solemnly stepped forward toward the Grand Master. His attire,

HER FRIENDS

composed of numerous shimmering and colorful fabrics, reflected his wisdom and authority over the galaxy.

He slowly raised his arms towards the heavens, as if seeking to invoke an invisible power. His eyes sparkled with a mystical light, as if they were the receptacles of ancient and profound knowledge.

Once his invocation was complete, he advanced toward the Grand Master, his eyes probing his soul. In a grave, prophetic voice, he uttered words that resonated in the air, carrying the promise of an inescapable fate.

"Lucian you were, and you shall be," he said, his voice resonating like a distant echo. "Lucian you were, and you shall be," chorused the other council members.

Lucian, once known as the all-powerful Grand Master, fell to his knees, his face hidden behind trembling hands. Burning tears, mixed with a thin stream of drool, flowed between his fingers, symbolizing his inexorable fall.

"What have I done wrong?" he pleaded, his voice shattered by the weight of his guilt. The power and authority he once possessed seemed to dissolve between his fingers.

"You have become evil itself," the council members replied in unison, their words filled with sadness and regret. "You are weak, Lucian. Power has consumed you."

Lucian shivered, dreading the punishment that awaited him. "What will my sentence be?" he murmured, his words heavy with anxiety and fear.

"A mortal existence in your own hell," they replied, accompanying their words with a gesture, pointing all toward the blue planet beyond the vast bay window. A planet that now symbolized his inescapable punishment.

A terrifying emotional shock crossed Lucian's face. He gazed at Earth with hatred, slowly realizing that he would be condemned to a normal life, devoid of power and domination, in this world he had sought to destroy.

"Who will take my place?" he whispered, his voice trembling with terror intertwined with a hint of despair.

The council members silently stepped aside, opening the arcane of their sacred formation, revealing Sara, who stood illuminated by the divine light of her destiny.

"The stars have birthed their most perfect being since time immemorial," explained the council elder, inviting Sara to step forward with a gesture of his hand. "She is the one who will lead us to the total energy of the universe," he concluded, drawing a large perfect circle in the air above her head. She illuminated the darkness of the metamorphosis unfolding in front of her, and she knew it. Her virtue had been recognized by the council, and she would now be the one to lead the journey of freedom and justice.

As Lucian gradually disintegrated into the air with an expression of infinite suffering, the council members escorted Sara to the throne in the grand hall.

The dean knelt on the ground, soon followed by all those present, in a rustle of garments resembling the ebb and flow of the oceans. Then, standing up, he brought a unique scepter to Sara. It was an exquisite work of art, finely carved from exotic wood and adorned with sparkling gemstones. Its centerpiece was a teardrop-shaped emerald, symbolizing wisdom and power. Sara received it with honor and sincerity, fully aware of the responsibility it represented.

"Great Mistress, take this scepter that we offer you. Always keep it close. It signifies the new era that belongs to you," the dean pleaded, almost as if in prayer.

Sara, feeling a bit awkward, thanked him with a smile full of kindness. Yet, one detail troubled her. But she didn't know how to express it.

HER FRIENDS

"Is something bothering you?" the dean asked, as if he were searching for a mistake he might have made.

"Yes. 'Great Mistress,' doesn't that sound a bit too pompous?" she admitted, feeling both confused and mischievous.

"Your name is of your choosing," the dean informed her, sharing a smile with her.

"Then call me... Sara!"

PAUL TOSKIAM

Fast Food

Sancho's Restaurant

"Lucian! What are you doing staring at the parking lot with your mouth hanging open?" Sancho, the fast-food manager, snapped. "I'm not paying you to gawk at the customers! Get back to your register and take the orders!"

Lucian, disheartened, shuffled his feet over to the counter where an impatient elderly customer was waiting.

"What does the old woman want? Can't she place her order at the kiosk like everyone else?"

The customer at the register, surprised and shocked, replied, "Oh, come now, you don't talk to a loyal customer like that!"

Lucian, disillusioned, leaned in closer to the elderly lady and asked with his predatory smile, "You still eat burgers at your age?"

Epilogue

Sara requested that the reconstruction of the Eiffel Tower be completed to its original design. She also proposed that the Great Pyramid be repositioned to its correct angle. Admiral Mobo, in his show of force, had misaligned it. "A soldier is not a surveyor!" she joked with him. Nevertheless, he took the necessary time for the reconstruction. He proposed a new, more elongated and taller design, along with better materials. Yet, in unison, the people demanded a restoration to the original state. He had to draw from his youthful archives in order to counterbalance the fright he had caused, fulfilling their wish. It was now ready to endure new millennia in perfect brilliance.

Sara warmly thanked Kurtz for paving the way to this destiny she had been unaware of. She made sure he had all the necessary resources to rebuild the Martian, ensuring it would be even more effective and useful than before.

She almost brought Lydia with her, who insisted on exploring the universe. However, her mother Justine managed to reason with her at the last moment by promising to buy her the latest phone of the year, with all the features. "Youth is fickle," Sara summarized kindly as she hugged them one last time.

George was weeping profusely in front of his daughter, shaking like an autumn leaf ready to detach from its tree. He knew he was looking into her eyes, her childlike eyes, for the last time. With his house reconstructed, he would lack for nothing. He apologized for taking so long to become the loving father she deserved. "This present moment is the greatest gift you could give me, Dad," she reassured him as she held him tightly in her arms one last time. Admiral Mobo stood beside them. She would soon be marrying him in an official ceremony.

The flagship soon left its orbit. Its red lights had given way to a blue aura, like that of Earth. The next time he returns here, this planet

HER FRIENDS

will have changed significantly. These events will be nothing more than moments in its history. They may become a forgotten chapter, buried in a memory that fades in infinite time.

THE END

Did you love *Her Friends*? Then you should read *The Fate of Lucian*[1] by Paul Toskiam!

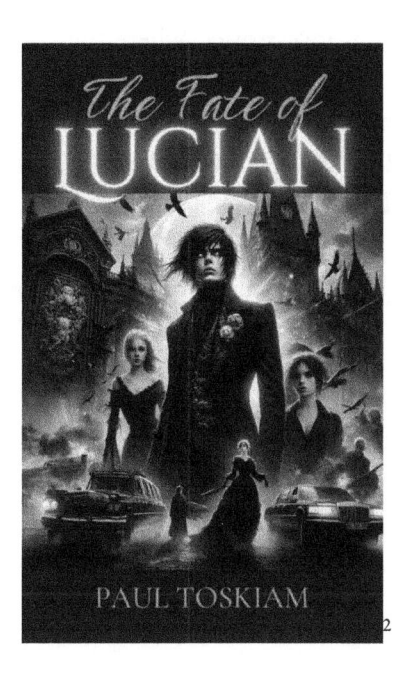

Carla and Sandra, two young friends in their twenties, are dining in one of the city's chic restaurants.

Soon Carla notices one of the customers staring at her.

He even leaves his table, where he's spending the evening with his entourage, to invite Carla and Sandra to join him at his house, where he's having a party **starting at midnight**.

The two friends don't know it yet, but Lucian has just drawn them into a world where **evil is a habit**.

How could such a harmless evening turn into a world where Carla and Sandra will lose all their bearings and have to fight to **save their lives** and the fate of the world?

---

1. https://books2read.com/u/3JB76K

2. https://books2read.com/u/3JB76K

Who is Lucian? What is his mysterious past? Why has he set his sights on Carla? Is she falling in love with **evil incarnate** in a **fiery inner battle**?

If you love magical love stories, where the **choices are difficult**, and above all, **irreversible**, then "The Fate of Lucian" will satisfy you beyond your expectations.

If you like **forbidden love stories**, **fantasy novels** and **psychological thrillers**, then "The Fate of Lucian" is for you.

Order your copy today and let yourself be seduced by this fascinating story that will shake up **your heart** and **your soul** like never before.

Also by Paul Toskiam

The Curse of Patosia Bay
Le bus de la peur
The fear bus
Elle mord les Zombies !
She Bites Zombies
No Treasure for the Brave
Pas de Trésor pour les Braves
Black Stone Hunter
Chasseur de Pierres Noires
Le Destin de Lucian
The Fate of Lucian
Her Friends

About the Author

Discover the captivating universe of PAUL TOSKIAM, the master of the extraordinary infiltrating the ordinary. With a voracious pleasure for turning mundane situations into thrilling adventures, he will make you reevaluate your certainties and completely shake up your perspective.

Forget about traditional patterns because with PAUL TOSKIAM, you will be drawn into extraordinary plots where tension is palpable on every page turned. The heroes and villains are not who you think they are. It's what will drive you crazy, but also what you'll love.

But that's not all, subtle and irresistible humor is one of PAUL TOSKIAM's trademarks. His characters come to life with realism, becoming endearing and unpredictable, adding a unique touch to each story.

Milton Keynes UK
Ingram Content Group UK Ltd.
UKHW020015061124
450708UK00001B/170